Knot of Christmas Past

Knot of Christmas Past

KNOT A CHRISTMAS CAROL

BOOK ONE

IMOGEN KNOWED

ISBN: 979-8-9874825-4-4

To everyone going through perimenopause, because it sucks almost as much as a heat without a pack of knots to make it all better.

Content Warnings

This book has explicit descriptions of sexual acts.

While all sex is consensual, some acts may be considered dubious or coerced.

There is mention of a past attempted sexual assault, but it is not described in any amount of detail.

CHAPTER 1
Evelyn

The unmistakable song of a video call interrupts me from my work. I roll my eyes and answer from my laptop, "Daddy, I have a bunch of important meetings I'm preparing for. I can't talk."

He nods, but ultimately ignores my plea to leave me alone. "Evelyn! Why are you working on Christmas Eve, darling?" He peers into the camera, as if he can somehow look into the 3D space and see around the corner.

"Because this is the last day to finalize some deals of Q4. Some things fell through, a few clients dragged their feet, and we had to line up some last-minute contracts, so..." I rub the bridge of my nose. "It just ended up being today. What do you need, Daddy?" I feel bad about my tone, but I asked him not to call me at work.

I suppose I'm not really supposed to be working today, so I shouldn't be so mad.

His eyes are soft and hopeful above his reading glasses. "I just wanted to know what time you and the pack are coming over tomorrow."

Shit. I forgot to tell them.

"I've been getting everything ready," Daddy giggles, sweeping the camera around so I can see the house. Christmas lights and other decorations are strung up behind him, covering the walls.

Dad's close-cropped head exits the view as he climbs a ladder in the background, holding a clump of string lights, and leaving his headless legs and wide torso visible.

Daddy sings, "Say 'hi' to your daughter, Patrick."

Dad's shoulders are hunched, annoyed as he unravels the string of lights, but he stoops so I can see his face. He waves and says, "Hi, honey."

Daddy smiles at him with all the love an omega can have for his alpha and says without breaking his gaze, "Your dad keeps joking he hasn't seen me running around like this since I was nesting when I was pregnant with you."

"I'm the one running around," Dad says back gruffly.

Daddy just tucks a strand of his red hair behind his ear and gives him the "you love it" look.

Fuck, how am I going to tell them? Just rip the band-aid off, Evie.

I swallow. "So, um...it'll just be me tomorrow, Daddy."

"What? Why?" Daddy asks, his gaze finally leaving Dad's ass, as he snaps his attention back to me.

"Jacob...he...he left. Took the pack with him. A few weeks ago."

"Oh, my...oh...Patrick, come here!" Daddy frantically waves Dad over to join him. "Oh, darling. I'm so sorry."

Dad enters the frame and puts his arm around Daddy's shoulder. "What's wrong?"

"Nothing's wrong, Dad!" I snap.

Dad's brow furrows, and he growls low and frustrated.

"Jacob left," Daddy whispers to Dad, stroking his arm. Dad softens immediately at his touch. "He took Mark and Lee with him."

Daddy continues his barrage of fatherly concern disguised as interrogation. "Are you okay, sweetheart? What happened? When did they leave?" He stiffens up, realizing what he's doing, and adds, "You don't have to talk about it if you don't want to, of course."

He says that, but the look he gives me indicates he'll continue to ask, just more covertly over the next few days, months, years, until he gets the full detailed carnage of the affair.

Tears threaten my eyes. I squeeze the bridge of my nose again. This mascara is waterproof, but I cannot risk looking like I've been crying all day. "Daddy, Dad, I'm fine. Jacob just couldn't handle my making more money than him."

Dad responds in his gruff voice, "He was weak. Didn't deserve you, anyway."

"I know, Dad." I repress an eye roll.

My mind flicks to the memory of my three alphas leaving me. Jacob said, "You'll be lucky if you find a single beta who wants an omega like you, let alone three alphas."

Daddy's voice goes soft and small. "Evie...sweetheart...Jacob didn't leave because he couldn't handle your ambition. He left because he didn't know how to be there for you while you outpaced him."

Damn, he's been practicing that one for a while. I guess I was the only one blindsided by Jacob leaving.

"Same difference," I sneer, and it's too late to take it back. The venom is real, but so is the ache underneath.

I'm snapping at them more than usual, and Daddy must notice, because he says, "Honey, you're looking a little...tired," in that way he does when he wants to ask me something, but doesn't want to set me off.

I ignore the question implicit in his gaze. "I'm fine, Daddy. Just... really working hard to—"

"Is that a nest?" Dad asks, having no qualms about setting me off.

Fuck. I didn't think they'd be able to see it. Damn these reflective, fucking glass walls.

I angle the camera away.

I risk a smile, but there's no sense in lying. "Just a little one." The admission hangs in the air, too light for the gravity of this moment.

"Why are you nesting in the office, sweetheart? Are your suppressants not working?" Daddy asks.

My gaze flicks to the couch in the far corner of my office, where the nest lives. "No reason," I say, even as my whole body shifts restlessly in the chair.

Last week, after I snapped at Bobby for likely the hundredth time in one day, then got all weepy over a stuffed animal, Bobby insisted that I set up a nest on-site, just in case.

But today, "just in case" feels more like "inevitable."

Dad glares at me, studying me. "You stopped taking your suppressants." He doesn't ask. He simply states a fact.

For a guy who doesn't say a lot, he sure does see a-fuck-lot.

I hesitate. The truth tastes metallic. "Yes," I say. "I stopped. It's not a big deal."

Daddy's eyes search mine for a second too long. He tries to restrain the panic obviously building in him and hangs on to Dad for emotional support. "It's a very big deal," Daddy says. "You haven't had a full heat alone in a very long time. Why did you stop your suppressants?"

"I just decided to." I don't want to explain that it's because my pack left me with parting words of how I'd been suppressing my heat for so long, I probably can't even go into heat anymore.

The cramp in my stomach sure fucking shows them. *Assholes.*

Daddy sighs, and I know he means it to sound empathetic, but it sounds judgmental. "Is it because Jac—"

"It's not about Jacob," I finish for him, mouth suddenly dry. My ex's name lands between us with a click, like a gun with the safety off. "I was due. It's fine. It isn't supposed to start until the New Year."

Dad sets his jaw, but doesn't challenge me.

Daddy's lips purse. "I just worry, honey. Withdrawal can be unpredictable, and—"

"I'm aware," I cut him off again, sharper than intended. My palm tingles where it's pressed too hard against the edge of the desk. "I'm not going to go through withdrawal. I stopped taking them under a doctor's supervision. I tapered off. I'll be fine."

Dad tightens up, restraining himself. He doesn't like that I keep cutting Daddy off.

My voice betrays my anger more than I wish it would. "I run a seven-figure company, and I'm a grown woman. I can handle a little hormone flux."

Daddy nearly pleads with me, "No one is questioning whether you can handle it. We just wish you'd take time off."

We? I hate when they talk about me through their bond like this. Dad is obviously losing his shit right now and letting Daddy be the bad guy.

I plaster on the most assuring smile I can muster. "I have three major client meetings today. If I close them, we double our market share by Q1." My voice wants to crack; I don't let it. "I can rest when I'm done."

Dad finally speaks up. "It's not safe for you to go into heat without an alpha to protect you." He stops himself from saying, "and knot you," because I know he's not particularly fond of thinking about that part when it comes to his little girl.

I reply, trying to ease his mind. "Dad, pretty much the whole company is off today. The building is practically empty. I'll be okay. It's just me, Bobby, and Tim. Even if I went into heat today, which I won't, they're both betas. I'll be fine."

"What about the three clients?" Dad asks.

Astute motherfucker. Can't ever get anything past him.

I sigh, there's no point in lying. "Only two are coming to the office...and, yes, they're alphas."

Dad growls, worried and annoyed at my tone. Daddy gasps and grips his arm, while he clutches his own chest. Dad softens, forgetting his own annoyance, and strokes Daddy's arm to soothe him. His purr is barely audible over the background noise cancellation filter, but I know he's doing it by the way Daddy almost melts into his arms.

I try to reassure them. "Listen, it's not going to happen for a few days. If the universe decides it truly wants to teach me a lesson and it happens today, I will go home immediately. My driver—a beta—will take me home and I'll be fine."

We're all quiet for a moment. In the silence, the faintest prickle of discomfort curls in my lower belly. I rub it, just once, as if that'll convince the sensation to behave until after 5 p.m.

Dad still won't drop it. "Is that Beta Admin of yours taking care of you, at least?"

"His name is Bob, Dad," I say. "Yes. He's the reason I have the nest here. He insisted I have it just in case. He's been scurrying around making sure I have everything I need to get through this. Alone."

"Good. That's smart," Dad nods authoritatively.

Daddy laughs, then turns serious. "You have a nest at home, too, though, right? Have you even been home recently?"

"Yes. Bobby helped me set up the nest at home, too." The words come out more defensive than intended.

"Is Bob going to help you through the heat?" Dad asks.

A smile tugs at my lips at the thought of Bobby pushing a vibrator with a fat knot into me, but I stamp it down. "Dad, that would be inappropriate, he's my employ—" A twinge cuts me off mid-sentence. I force my hands to stillness. The pain gives me a moment to realize Dad isn't asking if Bobby will take care of my sexual needs. He's asking if Bobby will help me stay hydrated and stop me from hurting myself if I get delirious with need. "Look, it's fine. I can handle it myself. I've done it before, and I can do it again. I have all the best nesting, hydration, and restraints money can buy."

Dad fixes me with a look that means business—half love, half domineering assessment. "You don't have to prove anything to us. Or to anyone." I know he's referencing my pack...ex-pack.

But that's the thing. I do. My whole life has just been a series of events in which I must prove myself. Prove that I can do anything a beta or an alpha can do.

Daddy knows this about me. He knows how much I resent being an omega and how hard I fight against the stereotypes. "I know you can handle it, honey, I do. You can handle anything," he says, voice barely more than a whisper. *Here comes the but:* "But, if it gets overwhelming, please promise you will call 4328. They'll send an emergency heat technician—"

I nod, throat tight. "I will. I've gotta go. Big day."

My fathers nod, then cut each other a glance that says they know there's no point arguing with me further.

They lean in together, and I catch the sliver of their hands overlapping just below the camera frame as they reach for the button together. It's a gesture so small, so sweet, it aches. "Love you, sweetheart," they say, in chorus.

"Love you, too," I say, and kill the call a fraction of a second early.

Power move, but hollow.

I sit in the silence, heart thumping, staring at the scattering of nest materials piled upon my office's couch and the floor in front of it. It looks so out of place against the glass-and-steel minimalism of my office: a soft thing in the middle of a hard place. *Just like me.*

CHAPTER 2
Evelyn

A slight knock, so familiar and reassuring, breaks me from my breathing exercises. I still haven't managed to get back to work.

"Come in," I say, trying to steady my voice.

The door opens with a polite click, and Bobby steps through, arms overloaded with bulging shopping bags. He pauses and scans my face for signs of imminent meltdown. When I don't bite his head off, he smiles warmly at me.

Bobby is always handsome, but something about today...

His white button-up shirt tucked into his black slacks accentuates his trim waist. His black hair falls into his eyes, crossing into the realm of his glasses. I imagine leaping over the desk, pushing him to the ground, and licking up the bridge of his nose, removing those glasses with the tip of my tongue.

Stop eye-fucking your employee, Evie.

"Bad time?" he asks, as he crosses the room, interpreting my lustful stare as annoyance, which is honestly a good read because I am annoyed by it. *I don't have time for this shit.*

"It's never a good time," I say gruffly.

"Was that your dads?"

"Yeah. They wanted to ask me about Christmas."

"They're excited to see you. It's been a while."

I feel like I should say "bah humbug" here, but that would be so cliché, I don't; instead, I just snort. He knows how much I dislike the holidays. He knows how much I dislike pretty much everything except video games and work.

He provides a tight, empathetic smile that makes me want to yell at him.

How dare he pity me!

I scowl.

He grimaces, but instead of apologizing, because he knows that will definitely set me off, he pulls out his phone and checks the time. "Your call with Elizabeth is in thirty minutes. If you can get her to keep it short, you should have a half-hour break before your call with Preston Geist."

My cheeks feel warm, but I can't tell if it's from the anxiety of the upcoming client meetings today or the creeping heat symptoms I refuse to acknowledge.

Bobby tilts his head, studying my posture. "Would you like some tea first? Chamomile. Or the black label anti-inflammatory stuff, if you need something stronger."

I don't want him to see how much I appreciate the offer. "Chamomile is fine."

He exits my office, and I inventory the nest in the corner. You'd think he was an omega by how good he is at preparing a nest. He's thought of everything. To appease him, I initially just threw a few crusty old blankets and a scarf from my youth on the couch. Refusing to cave to my instincts to create the softest pile of fluff and hide within it.

In the days since, Bobby had the blankets laundered to my usual specifications and has been adding layers: a few throws in a houndstooth pattern he somehow knew I'd find particularly appealing, a couple of accent cushions in my favorite color, and stuffed animals that match ones I had when I was a child.

Peaking out of the bags he just placed on the floor are even more nesting materials.

Bobby returns, holding two mugs. He offers me one. When our fingers brush, I'm shocked by how much I want to hold on.

I'm almost overwhelmed by the idea of dragging him into the nest, curling into his chest, and crying while he holds me.

He sits on the edge of the couch, practically in my nest already, and sips from his own cup. "Is it getting worse?"

"I'm fine," I say, but my voice sticks on the "f." I take a sip, trying to scald the honesty out of my mouth.

Bobby lets the silence grow comfortable. "I took the liberty of picking up some new nesting materials," he says, in the soothing voice he always uses with me.

I let my gaze drop to the bags I've been pretending to ignore since he returned. "You didn't have to—"

"I know," he interrupts gently, "But as your assistant, I know how often you sacrifice your personal needs for work."

I freeze. Anger surges through me.

How dare he think I'm some weak thing that needs help?

I snap, "I've gone through a heat before. I can take care of myself."

Bobby doesn't flinch. "I know. But you don't have to."

I set down my mug, careful not to spill. "Yes, I do," I say, my voice icier.

He just nods. Then, as if the moment needs a reset, he reaches into a bag and pulls out a softly folded blanket with a pattern of super cute foxes.

I seeth with rage at how fucking adorable it is and how he knows me so well. I want to rip his fucking head off...then kiss it.

"May I?" He gestures to the nest.

"Go ahead," I say, and watch as he layers it with surprising grace, fluffing pillows, tucking corners, engineering comfort. There's something almost reverent in how he handles the materials—like he's making something that will hold his most prized possession.

When he bends over to tuck the blanket, the way his pants stretch over his ass sends a new wave of heat through me.

I wonder what his dick tastes like.

Fuck, Evie, get ahold of yourself. You can't let this control you.

My laptop chirps, announcing another call.

I groan, putting my face in my hands. I don't even need to look at the screens. I know who it is.

"It's your fathers," Bobby says. He stands still, waiting for permission to answer the call, or for me to hurl my laptop across the room, perhaps.

I just nod, face still hidden in my hands, and he accepts the connection, answering from the large display on the wall.

Daddy's face fills the screen, close enough to show the lines around his eyes. Dad is there, too.

"Hi, baby," Daddy says, his voice wet around the edges. "We're so sorry to bother you again. We just wanted to make sure you had security in place at your apartment."

I look to Bobby, who's resumed smoothing the nest. "I've arranged for after-hours security to patrol her residence," he says, seamlessly assuming spokesperson status. "I've also ensured her nest at home has all the essential items. She should be comfortable, safe, and hydrated."

Daddy's relief is visible. "Thank you, Bob."

Dad asks, "Will you be staying with her, if she—?" He doesn't finish.

God, this is so embarrassing. They're treating me like a child, not a fucking leader of a billion-dollar company.

"If she needs me, I'll stay as long as required," Bobby replies. He doesn't look at me, but I feel a twist of lust and gratitude in my chest.

Is he offering to...? No...that can't be what he means.

Bobby's voice loses a bit of confidence, just slightly. "But Evelyn has made it clear she wants privacy and control."

I squeeze my legs at the thought of Bobby assisting me in more ways than just safety and hydration.

Dad smiles, tight but genuine. "She always was stubborn."

I resist the urge to correct him—*determined, not stubborn*—but my tongue feels lazy, thick.

Daddy leans in. "Evie, it's been a long time since you've gone into heat without an alpha. And you've been on suppressants for so long, this might be worse than you remember. Don't try to win at this."

Dad barks, "Just let it be what it is. Let Bob help you."

My head nods before I tell it to. "Okay."

Bobby looks at me and blushes, his face registering an emotion I don't quite know how to read. He then hurries to busy himself, taking that as a cue to unpack the rest of the bags. He places some flameless, scent-neutralizing candles around the nest as if he's preparing an altar.

Daddy says, "We'll let you go. Thank you for taking care of our girl, Bob."

"Of course," Bobby says, avoiding eye contact with me but looking at my fathers.

The call ends. The office falls silent, save for the hum of recycled air and fluorescent lights.

Bobby collects the shopping detritus, deposits it in the recycling, and returns. "Would you like to try the nest now, or wait until the symptoms...escalate?"

He knows as well as I do that I'm in pre-heat. I'm fooling no one with my insistence that my heat won't arrive for another week.

I glance at my watch. "Now is good," I admit. I remove my shoes, leaving them under my desk, and approach the nest.

Bobby holds out a hand, steady and unhurried. I hesitate for a moment and lock eyes with him. I accept his hand and let him help me lower into the nest. I sink into the mass of bedding, and for the first time all day, my muscles let go.

It feels kind of nice to let him help me.

"Let me know if you need adjustments," Bobby says, hovering a few feet away, awaiting my next move.

"I'm good. Thank you, Bobby." I close my eyes, feeling the world narrow to warmth and pressure and the faint, clean smell of new fabric...and cinnamon.

Bobby slowly backs away to the door, as if he's in the presence of a wild animal whom he can't turn his back on. He stops at the entrance, flips the switch that dims the lights, and lowers the blinds of the glass walls.

Oh, wow. I didn't realize how bright and loud those lights were.

I sink deeper into the nest, letting it cradle me and protect me from the reality outside my body. I close my eyes and for the first time in a few hours, I don't feel like I want to destroy the world...or fuck it.

Bobby says, just above a whisper, but loud enough to crack through my cocoon, "I will leave you to rest. Unless...unless you want company."

I open one eye and peer at him.

I want him to snuggle with me in the nest.

I want to sit on his face as his gentle eyes look at me the way they always do.

"Just...stay close," I say. And, not wanting to admit vulnerability or desire, I add, "In case I need more tea or something."

He closes the door, blocking out the last bit of light, and perches on the side of my nest—just out of reach, but present. Somehow, his presence feels like a warm hug.

For a few minutes, we're both quiet. My mind drifts, untethered for the first time all morning.

The ache in my belly is a steady pulse now, not a jagged warning, and I find myself clutching the new blanket with both hands.

A sharp spike of pain surprises me, eliciting a whimper. I am immediately embarrassed by my reaction.

Bobby clears his throat, then says, "I don't have a knot, but I'd be more than happy to—"

"Absolutely not, Bobby," I whisper.

I peek at him and, for a moment, I think he looks as if he may cry. A frown mars his usual calm expression. When he sees me looking at him, his face returns to normal. I...I don't want to ever see him frown like that again.

He's not sad, Evie. He's just doing his job. He's likely relieved he doesn't have to fuck the ice queen to keep his job.

But...just in case...I add, "That is incredibly generous, but you do not have to do that. HR would have my head."

He smiles, shifting his weight so that his body faces mine. "It would be my pleasure to assist you in any way, Evelyn." He emphasizes the word any.

The way he looks at me burns through me. It sends waves of heat and pleasure through my core.

My hands threaten to drift to the space between my legs, which is currently screaming, slick with need.

I swallow—hard. "Bobby, I—"

A bell on my computer alerts me to an upcoming meeting.

Saved by the bell.

"Um...Bobby, I have to meet with Elizabeth."

He stands. "I will be outside when you decide you need my help." He helps me stand, and when I reach my full height, his breath lands on my neck. It takes every ounce of willpower within me not to grab him, throw him into my nest, and rub my scent all over him.

My breath hitches. Our faces are so close we could kiss.

I lick my lips, feeling suddenly parched.

My voice comes out so breathy that he wouldn't be able to hear me if he weren't so close. "Thank you, Bobby."

He nods and then goes to leave. Before he can close the door behind him, I say, "Bobby..."

"Yes, Evelyn."

Stay. Hold me. Love me. Tell me I'm pretty.

His eyes are alight with what I initially interpret as hope, but dismiss as fear.

I straighten up, rebutton my blazer, and tug down my skirt before saying, "Can you turn on the lights?"

"Sure, boss," he says softly, before turning on the lights.

I blink as my eyes adjust, and I'm not sure, but I think maybe he looks disappointed.

CHAPTER 3
Evelyn

I flop back in my desk chair, jostling the mug of cold chamomile and not bothering to put my heels back on.

I log into the meeting, and Elizabeth Styles, whom I call Styles, my CTO and the lead programmer of the *Torchbearer* project, is already mid-glare. She's got a black gaming t-shirt under a fuzzy pink bathrobe: a dissonance she wears with purpose.

Her thick glasses reflect my own haggard image back at me.

"You're late," Styles says, no preamble.

"Lost track of time," I lie. "Sorry." *Also a lie.*

Styles snorts. "That's not like you." She glares at me, inspecting me with a precision only she is capable of.

"You nesting?" she asks, and I'm not sure what tipped her off. I ensured the nest was no longer reflecting off the glass wall behind me.

"Um...yeah, I kinda was."

"People always underestimate how much an omega can get done from a horizontal position." She doesn't smile, but there's a glint of solidarity in the comment.

I'm still recovering from the horizontal comment when she says, "*Torchbearer* is ready for the alpha launch on January 5th. Since everyone on the dev and QA teams takes December off, we ensured it was stable weeks ago."

I simply nod.

Styles is always on top of shit and is responsible for a large part of this company's success. I hired her fifteen years ago, and together we have consistently exceeded expectations of omegas ever since.

When I asked her to be CTO, she said, "I value my free time too much to be chief of anything." Eventually, she accepted, but with the ability to work remotely and with what is likely the most generous vacation package any C-Suite has ever received. She's currently on some island somewhere, living her best heat-suppressed life, working only when she feels like it, but still getting more done than most people.

I pull out my tablet, ready to take notes. "Walk me through what I need to know for my meeting with Preston Geist later today."

She shares her screen. "I'll keep it short." She launches into a curt and overly technical explanation of the current status of *Torchbearer* and how to demo the alpha build to the client today.

Usually, I have no problem following her explanations, but today, I track only about sixty percent of them. The rest is lost to the steadily rising ache in my lower abdomen and animal insistence that throbs between my thighs, radiating outward and turning every other sense on high alert.

She mentions a dip in frame rate during a specific sequence and some other issues with the build that we can address during the beta phase. "...or we could delay the alpha," Styles concludes, arms folded.

Delay the alpha. The phrase lands with unwelcome double meaning, and a sharp bolt of heat spikes up my spine. I clench my legs under the desk, then realize Styles is watching with that all-knowing look of hers.

I try to redirect. "Delaying the alpha isn't an option. They've already got a big alpha release party planned in LA with the movie's actors. He'll be fine with the current state. He's eager for studio execs to get their hands on it. I doubt that a bunch of movie executives will even notice a dip in frame rate—" I wince, my hand shooting to my side.

She tilts her head, calculating. "You okay?" she asks. "You look...like shit." Never one to sugarcoat anything: it's why I love her...usually.

"I'm fine."

Her eyes narrow. "Omegas just off suppressants always think they can ride it out. You're not the first to get caught off-guard."

I bristle at the implication.

How does she always ascertain everything going on with me? I didn't tell her I stopped my suppressants.

"I can handle it," I say, channeling my best CEO edge.

Styles raises an eyebrow, then softens—just a hair. "You don't have to handle it alone. There's a reason all the legacy corps used to assign a minder for this."

I want to tell her that I have Bobby, that he's better than a minder—he's a friend, a caretaker, a shield against the worst of it. But I also don't want to admit that I am, in fact, losing to my own biochemistry.

There's also a reason all the legacy corps never had omega C-suits.

She'd understand, though. I could admit it to her of all people...

Instead, I say, "I've got this."

Styles gives a tight nod. She hesitates, then adds, "I'm going to send you some documentation. I have a protocol I've been perfecting over the years, and I've automated everything related to managing my heat. Now that you don't have an alpha, it'll be helpful. You might not have time to order the necessary equipment, but it will still be of value."

I imagine Styles riding out her heat with a whole pack of automated robot alphas she's built specifically so she never has to interact with an actual human.

"Thanks, Styles," I say, though I know I likely won't take whatever advice she has.

"Give 'em hell, E," she says, indicating she wants to get off this call with me, and giving me a two-finger wave.

"You, too," I say, mimicking the gesture.

The meeting ends without any further fanfare. I stare at my hollow-eyed reflection on the black screen, then at the faint handprint I've left on the desktop from where I've been gripping the surface.

It's worse when I stand. The blood rushes everywhere at once, and for a terrifying second, I'm actually dizzy—real, full-body vertigo. The world tilts, my knees threaten to buckle, and I lurch toward the window for support.

Outside, the Minneapolis skyline is shrouded in white and blurred to anonymity by flurries of snow. A few floors below, the lights in other offices flicker through the cloud of flakes.

I peel off my blazer, which feels like a straitjacket, and let it drop to the floor. My silk blouse is half-untucked, damp from sweat, and clinging to every curve in a way that would mortify my fathers and amuse my ex. I tug at the buttons, open the collar for air, and try to breathe through the next round of cramps.

I just need to make it to 5 p.m. I glance at my watch. It's not even 9:30 a.m. yet.

It's no use. The pressure is building—hot, insistent, and so fucking unfair.

I should be able to muscle through this. I've handled worse: public speaking at launch events, crisis mediation with hostile investors, even a pack breakup on the same day a bunch of servers melted down.

But this is chemical, ancient, written into my marrow.

Unfightable.

The thought makes me furious.

The nest beckons, promising relief, but I can't bear the idea of curling up and admitting defeat.

Instead, I pace the room barefoot with my hands fisted at my sides.

A faint scent hits me. I look around, trying to determine its source. But I can't pinpoint it. It's ephemeral: a shifting undertone in the air, subtle and unfamiliar. I grasp to place it. Not just in location but also to pinpoint precisely what it is...*candy cane? Yes. It's a candy cane.*

God, this heat is driving me crazy. Now I'm smelling phantom candy.

I drop into my office chair, legs spread for balance, and tap at my phone, half out of habit. There's a string of unread texts from Bobby:

BOBBY

Do you want more tea?

The fridge is fully stocked with electrolyte-enhanced water.

Preston Geist meeting in 45.

I ignore them, focusing instead on the one message I want but will never get: a groveling apology from Jacob. A promise to come back. A regretful admission that he was wrong.

No such message exists. I stare at our last text exchange.

EVELYN

Working late tonight

JACOB

My fingers move of their own accord, opening a locked folder. Pictures of my pack—Jacob, Mark, and Lee—smile back at me.

We were so happy once. Weren't we?

I swipe forward a few images until I get to the ones I want: Jacob's knot buried deep within me.

I scroll through thumbnails—each increasingly more lewd, but none of them appealing, not really. The ache between my legs is a steady drumbeat now, and ignoring it just feels like martyrdom at this point.

I open the web browser and type "alpha and omega heat knotting."

I pick a video at random: an alpha and an omega tangled together. It's rough and somehow gentle. The wet sounds of the alpha rubbing the omega's clit would usually make me cringe, but right now, it triggers waves of slick to practically gush from me.

I slide a hand under my waistband, fingers finding heat and wetness. The feeling is so intense I gasp out loud. The sound echoes in the high-ceilinged office. I freeze, half-horrified, half-uncaring.

The omega whines, begging for the alpha's knot. I hold my breath, waiting for it myself. I angle my hand just so, grinding the heel of my palm into the ache, and let my head fall back against the chair.

The alpha purrs for her, and I can't recall the last time Jacob purred for me. *Had he ever?* The sound is so sweet and comforting, but it does nothing for me but make me want to cry. I don't have time to lose myself to the loneliness; I barely have time to rub this out, so I mute the video and try to forget the thought.

I close my eyes and picture an alpha approaching me, cock hard. In my mind, the alpha isn't Jacob. He's taller, thinner, a shadow. He smells like a candy cane.

"Oh, you sweet thing, why are you so sad?" he says, and I don't respond; I just rub faster. Angrier.

I imagine him purring, and it's so real that I have to check the phone to make sure it's still muted.

I realize I've been crying, and I can almost feel a callused thumb brushing a tear from my cheek as the alpha presses his bobbing tip against my lips.

"Be a good girl and open up for me," he says, and I do as I'm told. A faint wisp of candy cane teases my tongue as I imagine his precum dripping for me.

His shadowed hands know exactly where to press, when to pause. My imagination is so vivid, I can't distinguish between my hands and these phantom, alpha hands.

It feels so real.

He doesn't fumble or hesitate—just takes in a way that shows he knows exactly what I need. Like he knows all my deepest secrets and desires. He presses his cock deep down my throat, and I almost choke.

"Such a good girl," he growls into my ear.

His face is never clear, always half-turned, a mystery that makes the fantasy safe. But for a moment, I see a flash of a skeletal smile.

He drags his hand from my slick, up my chest, leaving a streak on my silk blouse, before pushing his finger into my mouth along with his fat cock.

My own gingerbread scent perfumes out of me, mingling with this overwhelming candy cane, reminding me of cookies I used to bake before I hated Christmas.

"You take me so well," the deep phantasmal voice whispers into my ear as my first orgasm washes over me.

I swear I actually taste candy cane spurting into my mouth in waves and coating the back of my throat as I hear, "Such a pretty little thing. I'm coming for you."

CHAPTER 4
Bob

It's been ten minutes since her call ended with Styles. Forty since she stopped answering my check-in messages.

I busy myself with tasks: rearranging the snack shelf, wiping down the kettle, and triple-checking today's calendar. But I'm not fooling anyone, least of all myself. Not that there's anyone here to fool.

A muffled moan, low and raw, bleeds out through the silence. I freeze, hands locked around a box of electrolyte water bottles, pulse spiking in my temples.

The blinds are drawn. The door is closed. Doesn't matter. I can hear it.

I pace in front of her door—a nervous animal in a cage—except I'm outside it.

I should go in. I want to go in.

But I know the drill: unless she asks for it, I can't help. She hates when her biology wins out. I've been with her long enough to know that. It's been years since she last let herself go into heat, but I remember it well. At least she had that mush-for-brains alpha to help her the last time.

I sit at my desk and turn on my computer.

She'll text if she needs something.

Maybe.

The moan comes again, sharper this time, riding a breath that sounds almost like a sob. *A whine.*

It shouldn't do things to me, but it does.

An omega whine isn't supposed to affect me. I'm a beta. But it lassos around my heart and pulls me right toward her.

I stand. Then compose myself and sit back down.

I stare right through my monitor, seeing nothing, and drag the mouse aimlessly through open windows.

I planned to triple-check the rota for her heat cycle coverage. It's an elaborate ballet of food and hydration deliveries, medical check-ins, and security sweeps. But every time I try to concentrate, my body tugs me back to that strangled, animal soundtrack.

The muffled rhythm of her whimpers is punctuated by an occasional irregular thump. Palms gripping her desk? Knees knocking the wood as she spreads her legs wide, pleasing herself? But worst of all are the sharp gasps that crack through the air like gunshots and shoot blood straight to the tip of my dick.

Maybe I can't really hear it. Maybe I'm just imagining it.

It's not just the noise. The scent is subtler, drifting through the HVAC in a way no filter can fully kill. It's sweet: gingerbread. I've been around enough omegas who went into heat to know what it means, but this is worse, because it's her. Most omega scents don't affect me. But Evelyn's scent calls to me, deep and primal.

I reach for the stress ball and squeeze it until my knuckles hurt. It doesn't help.

The urge to help is overwhelming, so strong that I have to grip the arms of my chair to keep from sprinting to her.

This is normal: empathy, not obsession.

I'd do the same for any omega in distress.

But that's a lie. This isn't about hydration. This isn't helping my boss to ensure I get a nice, fat Christmas bonus for my extra efforts.

This is about lust.

This is about love.

It's Evelyn. It's always Evelyn.

Evelyn is everything.

I have been in love with her for ten years, seven months, and (today) four days. Not that I'd ever say it. Not that she'd ever want me to.

Another cry: higher, then abruptly cut off. The silence that follows is even worse, loaded with images I can't help but picture: her curled in the nest I helped her build, back arched in pain, finding comfort in the fact my scent is all over it.

Or maybe she's face down on her desk, white-knuckling her way through another heat surge, and I'm behind her, pressing my dick into her slick heat, nuzzling into her neck.

It would be easier if I didn't care so much—if I could just treat her like a boss. But that's never been my gift. My gift is noticing. My gift is tracking every fluctuation in her mood, every spike in her cortisol levels, every new line around her eyes. My gift is knowing exactly when to intervene and when to leave her alone with her pride.

That fucking Jacob never appreciated how fucking perfect she was. He didn't care about taking care of her. He just cared about getting his rut out...and spending her money.

Mark and Lee were a little better, but they followed his lead. They were a pack before they met Evelyn, so their loyalty never lay with her...it lay with him.

Back before she started taking suppressants so heavily, I would send Jacob detailed spreadsheets explaining her mood, what she liked, and how to help her through it. But my messages would remain unread, and she'd come back from her heat break looking unsatisfied and unrested. I desperately wanted to be their beta. Her beta. But they didn't find my information helpful.

They didn't want me.

She didn't want me...

There's a new sound, sudden and sharp: a whimper, then a curse. My heart stutters. I want to go to her, knock gently, and ask if she needs water or a cold pack. She'd hate me for it. She'd hate herself for needing it.

I close my eyes and let my head fall into my hands. The memory of her from this morning is still raw: hair mussed, voice raw from suppressed emotion, fingers gripped tight around a coffee mug. The sight made my chest ache with love and very old hope.

A flicker of vulnerability. A flicker of softness. She let me see it. She dropped her mask for me for just a second, and I had to turn away from her so she didn't see the raging erection it caused.

The truth is, I'd do anything for her. Even this—sitting at my desk, listening to her writhe in pain and pleasure, while my own body reacts in ways that embarrass and baffle me.

I'm a beta. An omega's heat is not supposed to hit me this hard. But maybe I've spent too long in her orbit, and my wiring is all wrong now. Until I met her, I never fantasized about being an alpha. But I do now—constantly. I hate my own biology just as much as she hates hers, but for entirely different reasons.

I wish I could be an alpha right now. Slam open the door and slam my fat cock into her. Knot her so fucking good that her eyes roll behind her head, all while telling her about her upcoming schedule. "Oh, thank you, Bobby, you take such good care of me," she'd say. And I'd reply, "No prob, boss," in my much deeper, alpha-ier voice.

My dick is hard enough to hurt, and her scent is buried so deep inside of me I can almost feel it filling my lungs. We have state-of-the-art HVAC meant to filter it, but...*maybe the filters need replacing?*

I open a spreadsheet on my computer. The filters don't need changing, and it's not due for a cleaning.

Maybe her heat is surging more than it usually would due to the suppressant withdrawal she insists she isn't experiencing—despite the doctors telling her the chances of her having symptoms of withdrawal were high, even with the tapering.

Should I message her doctors? No, it's a holiday, and only crazy workaholics and their lovelorn assistants are working today.

The tension pools in my groin, slow and insistent. I fight it for as long as I can, but every new gasp from the office makes it worse.

I consider going to the men's room, but the idea of leaving her alone, even for a minute, is unbearable. *What if she needs me?*

I slide lower in my chair so that my waist is covered by my desk, and turn so that the security cameras don't have a shot of what I'm about to do.

I finally slide my hand down, half in shame, half in defiance, and press against the ache bulging in my pants. The relief is immediate, but it brings guilt with it, sharp and bright as a cut.

It's not perverse. It's biology. It's care. If I were in her pack, everyone would expect this kind of behavior from me. I'd get a work accommodation from HR allowing me to relieve myself as frequently as necessary whenever my omega went into heat.

But I'm not in her pack. I'm not her beta. I'm nothing but an employee. An assistant.

I just need to get it over with fast and keep it from interfering with work.

I bite the inside of my cheek, picturing the way she looked at me this morning. The way her eyes softened, just for a second, when she said, "Thank you, Bobby." The way she looked at me right before asking me to turn on the lights: like she wanted me to come to her, to comfort her.

I unzip my pants and release my cock from its prison. It unfurls, insistent, needy, and unfettered. The cold air against it somehow makes me even harder.

I picture Evelyn in her glass-walled office, shivering with need and fury. She's bent over her desk, crying as she attempts to pleasure herself. I enter the room, and her relief at seeing me is so overwhelming, she whimpers—for me. Not for an alpha. But for me. The man who loves her. The man who knows her better than she knows herself.

I embrace her, kissing away the tears, and tell her it will be alright. I will take care of her. I carry her to her nest and lay her down so gently that all her pain melts away.

In reality, I roll my thumb over the head of my cock, slicking myself with precum, wishing it were her slick, not mine.

I stroke, slow and careful, eyes fixed on the muted glass of her door, imagining the two of us together behind it. Her hair is mussed from sleep, her silk blouse is twisted around her ribs, revealing the underside of her breasts, and her lips are parted just enough to show her teeth. I slip my tongue in her mouth as my dick enters her slick, hot, pussy.

I imagine sliding my hand over the curve of her hips and burying my nose in her neck, getting to smell that gingerbread at the source. She'd moan my name as I bring her relief and pleasure.

I work myself with quick, silent strokes, my ass lifting from the chair as I try to fuck harder into my hand. The edge is so cruelly close, and I'm desperate for release.

My shame finally spills out of me in hot waves, and I catch it in my opposite hand. I lie here for a moment, staring at the fluorescent lights overhead, letting it burn into my retina, as my body regains its strength.

I grab a napkin out of my drawer and clean myself up. When I toss it into the bin, I feel even more hollow than I did before I came.

The muffled sounds from her office have faded to silence.

I check her calendar. She has twenty minutes until her meeting with Preston Geist. I hope she's finally getting a little sleep. Or finally able to work on some of the tasks she's been frantic to complete before the holidays.

I rehearse what I'll say when she finally opens the door for me: how I'll make her laugh if she seems like she's in a better mood, and how I'll never let her see how much I want her.

This is enough. Being close is enough. Helping in any way she lets me is enough.

CHAPTER 5
Evelyn

I blink, coming back to reality. The office is silent, save for my ragged breathing.

The bitterness is instant and total.

This is the life I built for myself: billionaire, innovator, lone omega in a tower of glass, masturbating between video calls and pretending it's enough.

I gather myself, stand, and walk to the window, where the city's lights twinkle through the snow. Somewhere out there, people are having real lives, real connections, real everything.

I touch my own reflection, fingers cold on the glass.

I can get through this. I'll prove them all wrong even if it kills me.

I clamp my arms across my chest and let my forehead fall on the glass with a thump. The pain is a slight relief from the sick loop of self-pity running through my head. I allow myself to purr for the first time in weeks, soothing myself as I watch my breath fog the glass in a growing circle of patheticness.

I should be prepping for the next call. But every nerve in my body is sparking, as if the air itself is composed of tiny pins meant to puncture me and me alone.

My skin feels too thin. My jaw aches from clenching.

I'm so supremely angry and so deeply sad.

And my fucking pussy is screaming for a thick knot to make it all better.

Traitorous bitch.

I look at the nest Bobby built for me, and I whimper. I want to wrap myself in it, form a cocoon, and vanish. Melt out of existence.

Instead, I drag my fingertips along the window until they squeak, drawing the Greek omega symbol in the fog.

It's so fucking unfair.

The window is cold against my forehead, but it does little to cool my overheating core. I press my whole body against the glass, hoping the cold from outside will seep through my bones. I consider unbuttoning my blouse and pressing my breasts against it, but I worry I'll be visible from the outside.

When I first started this company, the whole idea was to prove that omegas who didn't want to play the docile mascot, who didn't want to be someone's "little darling," could build empires all by themselves. I wanted to show that omegas didn't have to be "the omega behind the alpha." Show that omegas could take up just as much space as an alpha —metaphorically, at least.

And for the most part, I've done that. What I didn't consider was the fact that no alpha would want to be "the alpha behind the omega."

Now I'm packless, horny, and pressing myself against a cold glass window like some desperate, deranged, depressed, failure of biology.

I woke up this morning, and my hands reached for a presence that wasn't there. Jacob. Mark. Lee. All gone.

I should have just let them mark me.

I really shouldn't have offered to help fund Jacob's startup. That's where I really fucked up.

I should have just let them knock me up...

I let my head thunk gently against the window again. "You're being pathetic," I mutter, half-hoping the city below can hear me. "You're a CEO. You get paid to work, not to wallow."

I think about calling my dads, just to hear someone say my name softly. Hear someone call me baby, or honey, or some other term of endearment that makes me feel cherished. But I already know how it would go: concern followed by three rounds of "have you considered—"

I don't want pity. I don't need comfort.

My computer pings, sharp as a slap. It indicates I have ten minutes to get my shit together before my next meeting.

I don't move. Instead, I let my shit stay thoroughly un-together for just a little longer.

In ten seconds, you're going to get the fuck up and get the fuck over it. Stop being a little bitch, Evie.

I close my eyes and count backward from ten.

I force myself upright, shoving off the glass and rolling my neck until something pops. The ache in my pelvis flares, then settles into a low, electric hum.

I stroll to the closet hidden seamlessly in the walls of my office and push the wall to pop open the door. I pry it the rest of the way open to reveal a mirror and multiple changes of clothes.

I check my reflection. I look crazed. My hair is sticking out of my bun in a way that looks like someone was gripping both sides of my head, snaking their fingers through my hair, and loosening it from the elastic's hold. My blouse is drenched with sweat, and a slick mark runs up the front of it, as if I dragged a wet finger over it. *Did I do that?*

I remove my wet blouse and replace it with a nearly identical one from the closet.

I lift my skirt and step out of my soaked panties, replacing them with a pair of thick underwear designed to contain slick. When I smooth my pencil skirt back down, I turn to the side to check my ass.

Not bad. My butt looks a little bubblier, but that's definitely not a bad thing. I don't look like I'm wearing a diaper, which is good, because I kinda am.

I clean the corners of my eyes and mouth with a makeup-removing wipe, then reapply my mascara and lip gloss. I don't have time to do much else, even though the dark hollows under my eyes are in serious need of concealer.

I pull my hair out of the bun and run a brush through it. There's not enough time to put it back up. Down like this, it looks...more seductive than I prefer. Especially since I'll be meeting with an alpha, but there's no avoiding it now. Finally, I put my soiled clothes within scent-masking bags, then place them in the hamper.

I practice my smile: friendly, but not too friendly. It needs to be powerful, slightly cold. Preston Geist has become a friend of sorts in the year we have worked together. But I still need to maintain the facade, because he's still an alpha and I'm still an omega, and one slip from me will topple all the respect I've accumulated up to this point. And with him, slipping is more likely than any other.

He's an actor turned writer, director, and executive producer. He might not act anymore, but he still has the winning smile that got him lead roles in hit box office movies. A winning smile that will chip away at your guard and make you want to bend over for him: both figuratively and literally. It's disarmingly brilliant, and he's disarmingly charming.

I want to fuck him on a typical day. Today, when I want to fuck everything, I'm going to have to fight every cell in my body not to lick the monitor that projects his perfect visage.

Just over a year ago, he released the most successful superalpha movie of all time: *Torchbearer*. Then he came to us asking us to make his vision into a game.

We weren't his first studio of choice, though. He heard several pitches before ours. But they all pitched him the same trite, alpha-gaze bullshit. He'd almost given up hope of finding a studio that could make a game that understood what made the *Torchbearer* franchise so successful. Then he saw an article about me, played one of our games, and decided I was the one person who could do his game justice.

The thing that's made *Torchbearer* so successful isn't the abs, or the explosions, or the quippy dialogue. Yeah, sure, those help, but it's Torchbearer's flaws that make him a relatable hero. He's an alpha, he's a hero, but he's also a human, with weaknesses and feelings just like all of us. No other superalpha franchise had ever dared to show a non-perfect superalpha. He can shoot lasers from his eyes, and then he can cry. He can purr, fly, and then empathize with those around him. People resonated with that. Alphas, betas, and omegas all found things they loved about Torchbearer.

My omega-ness allowed me to see Torchbearer's vulnerability, and our pitch emphasized it. I saw that he was a man fighting against his alien biology, just like I fight with mine.

Preston was actually my first alpha client. Most alphas don't want the kind of games my company makes. We don't make games that tend to appeal to them: the kind that substitute machismo for substance. The kind that kill off omegas as a plot device to help the alpha lead grow into a better person or, at the very least, give him something to rage about. We make games that try to say something—try to make you feel things other than raging boners and, well, rage. Preston is one of the few alphas I've ever met who sees value in that.

My pack never got it either, and I'd be a liar if I said his appreciation of my work isn't extremely endearing.

Sexy as fuck.

My phone buzzes. Bobby's name, tiny and unobtrusive:

BOBBY

Five minutes, boss.

He's always ten steps ahead, always cushioning the world for me, and I know I'm lucky to have him.

I type back:

EVELYN

Thanks, Bobby.

My hand trembles. I flex it open and shut, watching the veins stand out.

I'm still replaying the moment from earlier: how I lost it, how the heat made my whole body stupid, how good it would have felt to have someone's weight pinning me down. Not Jacob's. Not even anyone in particular, just someone who could take the edge off. Someone who smelled like a candy cane and took what they wanted from me in a way that made me feel loved.

I wonder what Preston smells like. I wonder how he would feel breathing against the back of my neck as he held me so close our bodies literally fit together.

The shame is worse than the longing.

I wish I could want less.

I move to the desk and arrange everything in perfect order: monitor at twelve o'clock, water glass at nine, notebook at six, tablet at three.

I sit, back straight, hands folded.

For a second, I close my eyes and picture my old pack.

I wonder if they still think about me. I wonder if they miss my voice.

Probably not.

That life is lost to me now. I'll never be in a pack again, and that's okay. I don't need one.

I click on the "PRESTON GEIST (Torchbearer IP Holder)" calendar event.

CHAPTER 6

Preston

Most mornings, I'd start the day at the gym, crushing incline sprints before the world demanded my charisma. But today, I'm stuck in front of the mirror, fretting over my appearance. I've changed my shirt ten times, and now that I've finally settled on the one that brings out my eyes just right, I can't get these fucking cufflinks to cooperate. They're platinum, custom-engraved, and cost more than they have any right to —especially considering the fuckers are a real pain in the ass. *Shouldn't expensive shit be less of a hassle?*

They're a metaphor for my whole career, my whole life, really: expensive, one-of-a-kind, yet always a little off. Perfect until you get to know it.

Maybe I don't wear cufflinks—but that would mean I need a different shirt.

I groan, defeated, and continue to fiddle with them.

The hotel suite is the kind you only get when you're trying to impress someone. The floor-to-ceiling windows offer a panoramic view of downtown Minneapolis. Every surface is slick, touch-activated, and sterile. Mirrors cover so many surfaces, I wouldn't be surprised if this room has been the backdrop to some amateur pornos.

Maybe that's why everything smells of disinfectant. The room has to be hosed down after the massive orgies it frequently hosts.

I drop into the nearest chair and roll my eyes at the closest of my million reflections. I still look like a prince. The tailored suit, the sweep of my blond hair, the perfect line of my jaw: none of it accidental, all of it manufactured, none of it me. It's armor, curated and polished for effect.

But my hands...they betray me. They're a crack in the perfection facade. They shake, just a little, as I finally get the last cufflink into place.

It's not the meeting.

It's her.

It's Evelyn Charles.

The first time I met her was on a video call. I was expecting a nervous omega with a soft voice and something to prove. What I got was an ice queen in a blazer, whose voice could command a room without a bark, and somehow at a volume 10% of everyone else talking.

She bulldozed my negotiating team, then, when everything seemed settled, she had the balls to "circle back" and ask for royalties on any future sequels. I've closed bigger deals, but I've never left a call more wrecked. It was the fucking hottest thing that ever happened to me. I was rock hard the whole time. And now, after a year of creative meetings and late-night brainstorms, I'm sitting in a $6,000-a-night hotel suite five minutes away from her office, practicing how not to fuck up a thirty-minute video call with her, and wishing I had the balls to just go see her.

In two weeks, we will announce the first video game adaptation of *Torchbearer*. A lifetime's worth of box office and ego are on the line. But all I can think about is how this might be the last time I'll have a plausible reason to talk to her, to see her, to make her laugh with some offhand joke, to see the way her pupils dilate slightly when I flick my hair out of my eyes and grin.

I wonder if she ever thinks about me the way I think about her: constantly and with the desperate, unrequited yearning of a tween who still thinks boobs feel like water balloons.

My phone buzzes. It's a picture of a beautiful woman with a note from my mom.

MOM

She's an actress. An omega. Needs an alpha.

I roll my eyes. My mom has been trying to get me to settle down for the last year. Since my dad died, all she can think about is grandpups. Every message I receive from her is an attempt to pack me up or hook me up with an omega. She can't understand the idea of an alpha not wanting an omega.

She's a beta. So was Dad. She'll never get it.

I dismiss the message, then pull up my notes for the call. These calls have been the most exciting part of my life over the last year. But it's not enough. I want more.

I do want an omega. I want Evelyn.

I want to know if she's seeing anyone. I want to know if she's as lonely in that glass office as I am in this 4,000-square-foot coffin. I want to know if there's any shot in hell she'd let me take her out, just once.

I picture her as she was on our last call. Her hair was up in a messy bun. She was wearing this dark, fitted button-down with the sleeves rolled up, revealing the delicate curve of her wrists. She had a silver chain around her neck that drew my eyes to her cleavage. Not that I needed anything to draw my eyes there. The buttons strained against her breasts, leaving a small pocket that threatened to offer me just a peek. When she said my name, it came out low and slow, as if she was tasting it before spitting it out.

I wonder how she'd say my name with my face buried in her cunt.

My dick presses hard against my pants, and my knot swells, wanting to lock into her. I check my watch to see if I have enough time to blow this load before I speak to her. *Clear my head by clearing my balls. All over her chest would be preferable.*

Three minutes.

Nope. Probably can't get it done that quickly.

I get up, cross the room, and lean against the window, watching the morning flurries bounce off the skyscrapers. There wasn't a hotel room close enough to her office that I could see her from my window. If there had been, I would have booked it, regardless of the cost.

Somewhere out there, she's in her own office preparing to meet with me.

I wonder if she's as nervous as I am.

Doubt it.

I shake myself, crack my knuckles, and rehearse sussing out if she's single, or at least looking for another alpha: "So, Ms. Charles, doing anything fun for the holidays?" *Lame. Too rehearsed.* I try again: "Got any plans for the holidays? Getting triple-dicked by a whole pack of alphas, perhaps? Got room for one more?" *Obviously, I can't say that.* "I usually go skiing in Valle. Alone. How about you? Oh, you're alone, too? How about we be alone together?" *Not even marginally better.*

I'll wing it.

I glance at my watch again. One minute until call time. I refuse to be late for her. Punctuality is one of those small gestures that show her I care—that I'm not just another arrogant bastard who thinks she's disposable.

I check my hair one last time, then the backdrop—the president's suite of the most expensive hotel in her city. Maybe she'll notice I'm here. Maybe she'll recognize the room and offer to come here. Be so turned on by the idea of my proximity and obvious show of wealth, she'll come over here, blow me, and we'll live happily ever after, with me knot deep in her for the rest of our lives. Have about 30 pups who are also creative geniuses and finally get my mom off my back.

I groan.

She won't give an absolute shit. She's richer than I am.

How does an alpha seduce an omega that already has everything?

I sit, square my shoulders, and log in to the meeting. It shows she's already on the call. I click connect, and it takes longer than usual to pop the video feeds into place. For a second, I panic that the connection's going to drop and that all this buildup will be stamped out by shitty hotel wifi.

The video flickers to life, and there she is...Evelyn.

I nearly swoon.

Her hair is down, damp around her face, framing it in uneven waves. She looks how I imagine she would right after she's taken my knot and is basking in the afterglow of my love.

Her eyes feel like they lock with mine momentarily, which I know is impossible to determine over a video call, but for a heartbeat, I feel naked, vulnerable, seen.

Showtime.

I smile, real and wide. With a voice I reserve for interviews and her, I say, "Good morning, Ms. Charles!"

God, I sound like a schoolboy with a crush on his teacher.

She smiles tightly. "Good morning, Mr. Geist."

I fiddle nervously with my cufflinks in my lap, just out of her eyeshot. "Any chance you'll be coming to LA for the launch event?" I ask, as casually as I can manage.

She hesitates, just long enough to make my heart stutter. "Doubtful. That's not really my scene."

It stings, but I like it. I like it when she's real with me. It's not often, but occasionally she will drop the professional power bitch facade and corporate lingo and be a real person. As much as the ice queen with her shit together turns me on, the perpetually tired, sarcastic woman who has too much shit to do, to deal with my shit is even hotter.

I nod, pretending I expected the rejection. "If you change your mind, I could show you the best rooftop in the city. They've got a view of the whole skyline, plus a private chef. I could introduce you to the cast of the movie."

She stops me with a look. Not unkind, just tired. "I wouldn't really fit in."

"Of course you would. You'd be with me."

She considers me for a moment, and I think she may actually accept. But instead she says, "I've actually got other plans. Sorry."

Strike out. Yet again.

"Understood," I say, not letting the defeat show on my face.

I know what she thinks. That I'm just a vapid Lothario. A packless alpha who ruts his way through a slew of nameless hotties. And, in a sense, she wouldn't be wrong.

Every few weeks, a new article comes out claiming I'm hooking up with some high-profile omega or canoodling with a bonded pair who need an extra knot for a heat cycle. It's almost always untrue.

Don't get me wrong, I've definitely gone on a few rut sabbaticals, forgoing my suppressants for a weekend, high on ecstasy and hormones, while shoving my knot in everything that moved. But that was decades ago, when I was young and didn't work eighty-hour weeks.

The tabloids aren't entirely wrong in their assessment of me. I've dated, but never seriously. I've probably broken more hearts than I will ever admit to myself. But I'm not a rolling stone. I know it sounds cliché, but I've just been waiting for the right woman—the right omega.

And I've found her.

Unfortunately, she lives two time zones away and scares the shit out of me.

I want to tell her that I'm not just looking for a rutting good time with her. That I'd actually take care of her. I want to spend the rest of my life trying to win her favor. I want to protect her. I want to get the fuck out of her way and let her protect herself, because I know that's what she wants.

She's the first omega I've ever wanted to show my true self to, not just the version I created for the cameras. And she's the first omega I've ever wanted to learn about: really learn about. I want to know every flaw, every fear, every imperfection. And I want to wrap every one of those imperfections up in my arms and tell them how perfect they are anyway.

I pull at my stupid fucking cufflink, which has somehow clicked out of place, and I ready myself to really ask her out. No pretense. No ruse. Just spill my guts. Seize the fucking day because this might be the last fucking one. But she's already gone: mentally. Her eyes are drifting to a different part of the monitor as she prepares whatever it is she's going to show me.

I missed my chance.

She sighs, deep and uncharacteristically unguarded. "Let's get on with this."

"Yeah, sure," I say, and force a smile.

CHAPTER 7
Evelyn

He looks annoyingly perfect, as always—blond hair waving just right, just enough shadow along the jaw to remind you he's a wolf underneath the suit.

Sometimes I wonder how he wrote *Torchbearer*. He doesn't seem to have a single flaw or vulnerability.

He's framed by a hotel room that is bigger than most of the apartments in this city.

My eyes linger on his Adam's apple. I imagine licking it. Sucking it into my mouth and leaving a purple mark in my wake.

I zone out for a moment.

"Ms. Charles, you still there?"

I shake my head, trying to wipe the daydream from my brain. "Oh, sorry."

"I thought the feed froze for a minute. Shitty hotel wifi, you know?"

"Ha, yeah, I know."

I click on the various icons on my desktop, forgetting what I had actually set out to do.

"Um..." I say, pulling out my phone, hoping it will have the answer, and the porn I was watching starts playing.

"Fuck," I nearly shriek, turning off the phone and slamming it face down, possibly cracking the screen.

Thank God the video was muted. I don't think he saw what was on the screen.

He leans back, laughs like he's sharing a private joke. "You alright? You seem a bit out of it today."

My first instinct is to lie. "Fine. Just running on caffeine and spite, like always." But the words taste rotten. The ache in my core intensifies, a hot fist that pulses up my spine, and I realize I'm holding myself rigid, like a wild animal waiting for the next blow.

He's still watching, head cocked. "Do you need to reschedule?"

The suggestion stings. "No. I said I'm fine," I snap, but the edge is dulled by the warble in my voice.

It's not lost on him. His smile drops. "Seriously, what's going on?"

I stare at my own hands, knuckles white on the desk. I could feed him the script—"Just a rough patch, we're all good, promise"—but something about the way he's looking at me cracks it all open. He and I have developed a casual friendship over the last year, and it weirdly feels wrong to lie to him. "Have you ever had one of those days where it feels like the whole universe is against you?" I blurt and immediately shake my head.

Fuck. I can't believe I just said that. Of course, he never feels like that. Look at him.

Silence.

For a second, I'm the one who thinks the connection has dropped this time.

But before I have a chance to say so, he says, "Every single day."

I look at him, surprised. I've never seen him so earnest.

"Sorry, Mr. Geist. That was...unprofessional of me. I'm just dealing with some...personal stuff."

He just watches me, waiting for me to continue, and it makes tears well in my eyes. I wipe one away. "Sorry, this is...I just need a minute."

His face changes, something hungry and dark flickering behind the eyes. "Who hurt you?" His voice is low, a growl pitched just above a whisper. "Tell me who. I will kill them."

The words land like a slap. I almost laugh; the urge to cry is reduced by the ridiculousness of it.

These alphas and their conclusion jumping.

"Don't be dramatic," I say, stifling a wince and a slight laugh. "It's not that kind of pain."

He sits up, more serious than I've ever seen him. "I'm not being dramatic, Ms. Charles. I need to know what's wrong."

I look past him, at the hotel room that seems vaguely familiar, and try to anchor myself. "I'm just having some health issues. It's not your problem."

His eyes widen, and for the first time since we met, he's rattled. Not for long—he regroups instantly, folds his hands, and puts the mask back on. "If you need to reschedule—"

"No," I say, a little too harshly. "We're on a deadline. Let's get it over with."

He opens his mouth like he's going to push back, but then just nods. The same way Dad does when he wants to bark at me, but he composes himself instead. "All right, Ms. Charles. Status update, then."

Styles explained how to do this. I just need to open the screen share software, turn on the controller, and then open the build. Easy.

I click the icon to open the screen sharing software, but nothing happens. It doesn't do anything.

I click again, harder.

What is wrong with this mother fucking piece of shit!?

My hands are shaking and I'm struggling to keep my grip on the mouse. Heat originating from my core climbs up my neck, creeping into my ears, and flushing my face.

"Technical issues?" he asks, a cool cucumber to my red-hot pepper.

"No, just..." I bite my lip and try to control my breathing. "Just a moment."

He waits. Unhurried. Patient. It should be calming, but the contrast with the pounding in my ears seems to inflame my panic. "Take your time," he says. "I'm not going anywhere."

My eyes sting again. I blink fast, determined not to cry in front of him.

I finally get the screen share to work; it was open in the fucking desktop tray, hidden from plain sight.

Fucking bullshit UI design.

Note to self: form a team dedicated to finding a different, better, screen share tool. If one doesn't exist, build it, put these motherfuckers out of business. Burn their shit to the fucking ground.

I click on the build.

Fuck. I was supposed to turn on the controller before opening the build.

I curse under my breath, then look up to see Preston watching every micro-movement. His face betrays nothing except perhaps a slight fascination. I'm sure he's enjoying seeing me spiral.

The omega who got too big for her slick containing britches finally falls from her ivory and glass tower.

The build launches, and I turn on the controller.

The game loads—our game, the one my team has dedicated over a year of their lives to—but the intro stutters, then freezes.

The avatar on screen mirrors me: locked in place, unable to proceed.

"Fuck!" I say a little too loudly.

Styles told me this would happen if I didn't turn the controller on before launching the build.

Fucking alpha builds and their fragility.

I want to throw my computer across the room. Instead, I slam the controller onto the desk and push away. My chair almost topples.

I'm humiliated. My body's revolting, and now I've made a spectacle of myself in front of the one client I can't afford to lose.

I stabilize myself on the desk and regain only a fraction of my composure. "I'm sorry," I whisper. "This is...This is wholly unprofessional."

There's a long pause.

"Evelyn." No title, no formality. Just my name, like he's been waiting all year to say it. "I'm in Minneapolis."

The words make something in my chest twist.

He's here? He's in my city?

I want to bite him, just to see if he bleeds. I want to wrap myself so tight around his cock that I squeeze the lifeforce out of that pretty face as he drains his balls into me.

Preston breathes, slow and measured, as if he can read my thoughts. "Let me come to you today and see the build in person. I've always wanted to see what the studio looks like."

I want to hang up.

I want to accept.

I want him to pound into me while I demo the build.

The pressure in my core is building. The ache is now a sharp, pulsing need that radiates out to every limb.

I almost fucking whimper at the thought of him coming to me.

Coming on me.

Coming in me.

I can feel my scent shifting—sweet, high, impossible to mask. If he were here, he'd know instantly I'm in heat, if he can't already tell.

I weigh my options.

I should reschedule.

I open my calendar. There's no time to reschedule. Not with the holidays coming up. My heat will probably run through the New Year. Since the release party is scheduled right after the holidays, today is literally the last day to show him the build before then.

I could call Styles and get her to show him.

Or...

I could let this alpha come to my office, show him the build...and maybe...

"Let me check my schedule," I say, pretending to scroll through my calendar, already knowing exactly where I can fit him in (pun fully intended).

My hands are steadier now, the anger stabilizing in me and replaced by pure, white hot lust.

Preston waits, mouth tight.

"There's a slot this afternoon," I say. "2 p.m."

He grins, a wolf's smile. "Perfect. See you then, Evelyn."

The call winds down, the usual wrap-up—"thanks for your time, see you soon"—but the tone is different now. He's all smiles again. Grinning like he just won some secret prize.

As soon as the screen goes dark, my body is overcome by intense heat. It's so intense my vision goes black for a moment, and I'm lucky I'm sitting, because I would have fallen otherwise.

Now I have not two, but three alphas coming into my office today.

Fuck. I'm screwed.

Hopefully...

CHAPTER 8
Evelyn

After the call, I sit motionless in my chair, eyes burning from the constant threat of tears today and something...hotter...

Preston's beautiful face is imprinted on my retinas, all sharp cheekbones and predatory charm. The image won't fade. It burns. The thought of the flirtatious, handsome alpha being in the same room as me makes me think I'll need to change my panties again very soon.

I tap my fingers against the desk, fast, trying to shake off the tremor in my spine. It's humiliating. I'm a grown woman. I'm supposed to be running a company, not having an out-of-body experience because a man called me by my first name. The way he said it made me want to crawl out of my clothes and right into his lap.

The meeting is closed, but it feels like he's still watching. I flip the cover on my camera, like I can suffocate the memory.

A soft, cautious knock. Bobby, of course. I call him in, and he opens the door just enough to peer at me through the crack, but not enough for me to hurl something at him through it. Once he confirms the coast is clear, he enters with his ever-present tablet and a stack of printouts. He knows when I'm pre-heat, I prefer to read things on paper as the light from monitors and screens can give me a migraine.

He gives me a look I can't quite read, and I wonder if he heard me earlier. If he had, he doesn't dwell on it; instead, he moves the day along just like always: my compass in a storm, pointing me where I need to go. "Tim will be in at 11 to go over his pitch before the meeting with Dr. Chris Yore," he says, low, neutral. He doesn't look up right away, just lays the stack on the desk and aligns the corners.

I nod, not trusting my voice. My head is pounding. I want to curl up in the nest and black out, but I settle for a polite, "That's fine."

"Your only other meeting is with Finn Future at 4:00. Do you want to review your talking points for that pitch or...?"

I zone out for a second, watching the shape of his hands as he sets his tablet on the desk and flicks at it. There's something gentle about the way he moves—efficient, but always deliberate, never rushed. Even the way he stands, always at an angle to the door, like he's ready to shield me from an intruder or slink away if I'm in a mood.

I realize I'm staring and snap my gaze to the calendar. A new entry pops into view as his copy of my schedule syncs:

> 2:00 p.m. – [ONSITE] PRESTON GEIST (Torchbearer IP Holder)

My stomach drops. I feel seen, like I've left a trail of pheromones and slick through the digital ether, and Bobby has just sniffed me out.

He looks up at me, blinking slowly. "That wasn't on the calendar this morning," he says, which is as close to "Did something happen on the call?" as he'll get.

I shift—uncomfortable, judged.

"I had a technical difficulty," I say, too fast. "I wasn't able to share the game's progress with him during our call, and he happens to be in town, so...he's coming into the office."

He looks at me a moment longer, as if waiting for a punchline, then back to the tablet. "I'll contact his assistant and see if I need to arrange transport. If you'd like me to sit in, just flag it."

I almost wish he'd chastise me. Call me a naughty girl and convince me to call the rest of the day off. But, I know it wouldn't matter, I've made my nest and I'm gonna lie in it.

I open my mouth to respond, but my mouth is suddenly too dry.

The heat is building again, not in slow increments but in a dizzying wave that makes the floor feel unstable. I reach for my water glass, knocking it over in my haste. A thin sheet of cold spreads across the surface, soaking the stack of printouts he brought me.

"Sorry," I mutter, dabbing at it with my sleeve.

He moves quickly, grabbing a cloth from his pocket and mopping it up with surprising grace. "You okay?" he asks, softer now.

I try to laugh, but it comes out like a cough. "I think my brain's overheating."

Bobby pauses, cloth in hand, and studies me. He's always careful not to crowd, but this time he lingers. "If you need to step out, I can reschedule—"

"I don't need to step out." The words are sharper than I intend. I regret it immediately, but I can't take it back. "I'm fine. Really."

I hate that I keep snapping at him. I hate that he keeps taking it with such a gentle, understanding stride.

He steps back, giving me space. "Of course. But if you do need anything—ice packs, electrolytes, or just a break—let me know. I'm here to assist in any way I can."

I nod, pretending to check my email, but my focus is shot. The top message is from THNTS.exe, pronounced either "Thantanos dot exe" or "Thantanos execute" depending on who you ask. It's the stage name of Finn Future, a DJ who's never confirmed how to pronounce it, because he's never uttered a word in public. No one has ever seen his face or heard his voice, and all of my correspondence with him so far has been via email only. But, for some reason unclear to me, he's decided to fly into Minneapolis from Paris to meet about a game we'll be collaborating on in the new year.

He made the soundtrack for the *Torchbearer* movie, and we were able to get him to bring his skill to the game, as well. It's been amazing working with him because his work has elevated the game to a level my team couldn't achieve on our own. I have talented artists and musicians working for me, but none can capture his particular sound, so getting him on the project was a real boon to its authenticity.

The original plan for *Torchbearer* was for him to work on the music alone, then send the finished files over. But, at some point, Styles explained the software we use to sync the music to the game, and he really took to it. Now he wants to collaborate on a game and work as a musician and engineer.

I stare at his email that provides the logistics of his arrival later this afternoon, but I'm having trouble parsing the words. They blur into a block of nonsense. I press my palms into my eye sockets and exhale.

Bobby's voice breaks through the fog in my head: "I can cancel the Preston Geist thing, if it's too much. Today's meeting was a courtesy—not necessary for the alpha release."

I drop my hands, fixing him with a glare. "I can handle a client meeting." I know what he's thinking: I shouldn't be around these alphas today. And I know he's right, but I add anyway, "Even with alphas."

He looks almost apologetic. "I know. It's just..." He trails off, uncertain. "This cycle is...more intense than the ones you had in the past."

I want to yell at him, tell him to stop treating me like a delicate thing, but I can't muster the energy. Instead, I slump in my chair and pull at my collar, trying to get air to my neck. The room is stifling.

Bobby watches, concern etched into every line of his face. "You're running hot," he says. "Let me get the fan?"

I wave a hand in permission, too exhausted to speak. He crosses the room, opens a hidden closet door, and pulls out a high-performance filtration floor fan. He positions it in the same careful, conscientious way he does everything: finding the perfect position and delicately placing it where he deems best. After he's satisfied with its proximity and angle relative to me, he stands in front of me, points the remote at the fan, and sets the speed at the highest setting. He's testing the air, blocking it from me, ensuring with his own body his calibrations are correct before letting it touch me—just like he does with everything.

My eyes water and sting at the realization. Bob is the only person who's ever put this much effort into ensuring my comfort, and I feel bad for taking it for granted, especially over the last few days.

He steps aside, letting the air hit me with full force, and a rush of cold air slaps me, bracing and sharp. I needed this so badly. He always knows exactly what I need. I unbutton the top buttons of my blouse—that I'll likely have to change out of again—and let the air hit my neck. But with it comes a scent—spicy, sweet, unmistakably cinnamon.

Bobby.

It's that unmistakable underlying note that must have always been there. Still, I just didn't really notice before—masked by suppressants, coffee, and the best pheromone filtering HVAC money can buy.

The smell is both grounding and destabilizing, and it somehow consumes all of my senses. I can feel it, see it, taste it.

The fan is meant to help filter out pheromones, but apparently, it does jack shit when a super pretty little soft boy stands in front of it. And God, the way the air is dancing his hair into his eyes and forcing his shirt to outline his body. I gulp.

He returns to my desk, careful to stay just outside my personal space. "Better?"

I nod, the taste of cinnamon on the back of my tongue making it feel fat. "Yeah. Thanks."

He hesitates, then takes a step closer. "Are you sure you don't want to—?"

I cut him off, voice low. "If you keep babying me, I'm going to start docking your pay."

He laughs, a soft, genuine sound. "But, boss, I have children to feed." *He doesn't.*

I laugh, and the tension in my neck eases. He always knows exactly what to say and do. Always.

I manage a weak smile. "Thanks for everything you do for me, Bobby, truly."

CHAPTER 9
Bob

She's looking at me in a way that makes me...uncomfortable isn't the word. She's sitting at her desk, hair falling softly over her shoulders, eyes red-rimmed but dry and locked on me in contemplation. It's almost like she's seeing me for the first time.

"Hey," I say, as gently as I can manage. "Would you like some tea?"

She looks at her hands flat on the desk. "I'm fine, Bob. You should go home. You weren't even supposed to come in today."

I ignore the order. "That's not happening. Not until you're okay."

She glances up, and for a second, the mask slips. I see the fear, the loneliness, the bone-deep exhaustion. It makes my chest ache.

I sit in the guest chair, give her space. "You want to talk about it?"

She shakes her head. "No. I want to forget I exist for ten minutes."

I nod, thinking.

I go to the fridge she has hidden in a wall under her television monitor and get a bottle of electrolyte water. I consider refilling her glass, but decide against it.

"Drink," I say. Not an order, just a suggestion.

She eyes the bottle like it might bite her, then takes it in both hands. She doesn't drink right away, just holds it, feeling the cold water against her skin.

"I'm sorry," she says, voice barely above a whisper.

"For what?"

She shrugs, staring at the bottle. "For being a mess. For making you deal with me."

I want to say: I'd deal with you every day for the rest of my life. Instead, I say, "You don't have to apologize. Not to me."

She snorts, a weak sound. "I do, though."

"It's why you pay me the big bucks," I joke.

She smiles, just a little. The heat in my chest ratchets up a notch, the way it always does when I make her smile.

I watch her for a minute, the way her shoulders curve, the way her wrists look so delicate and breakable. I want to reach across the desk and take her hand, but I don't. I never do. Instead, I say, "Can I ask you something?"

She lifts her head, wary. "What?"

"Did something happen during the client call?"

She stiffens, but then relaxes. "Well, I supremely fucked it up. I couldn't focus, and the build froze."

"Just a hiccup."

She shakes her head. "I can't have hiccups."

She's so hard on herself. She thinks if she's not perfect at all times, her entire empire is going to come tumbling down around her.

She sighs, then leans back in her chair, closing her eyes. "He just... He makes me feel like I'm not enough." I'm surprised by the admission.

I shake my head. "That's bullshit. You're more than enough."

She laughs, sharp and bitter. "Tell that to my ex. Exes."

I want to punch them, but I settle for saying, "He was an idiot. They were idiots."

We're both quiet. I feel like I'm standing on the edge of a cliff, one word away from free fall.

She finally takes a long sip of the water, and I can see the relief on her face.

She sets the water down, then looks up at me, eyes glassy as if she may cry. "Why are you here today? Why are you always so nice to me?"

The questions are so honest, so raw, it almost hurts. They crack me open and make me want to spill my guts at her feet. I want to admit every emotion I've been harboring for a decade. I want to tell her why, even if the paycheck stopped, I'd still be right here where I am: at her helm, steering her, helping her, loving her.

I take a breath, and then—before I can chicken out—I say, "Because I love you."

She blinks, surprised. "You...what?"

"I love you," I say, heart hammering.

She looks away, flustered. "That's...That's not appropriate. I'm your boss."

I walk around the desk to stand beside her. "I don't care. I've felt this way for a long time, and I'm tired of pretending."

She goes still, jaw working. I think she might tell me to leave, or fire me, or worse—laugh in my face. "What do you want?"

I don't hesitate. "I want you to let me take care of you."

She laughs again, but it's different this time—softer, sadder. "Bobby, you already take care of me."

"Maybe," I say. "But I want to do more."

She looks at me, really looks at me, and I see the struggle on her face. The part of her that wants to say yes, and the part that's terrified to need anyone.

She's about to speak when another wave of pain hits. I see it in the way her fingers spasm, the way her thighs clench under the desk. She bites her lip, hard, and I can't take it anymore.

I circle behind her and rest my hands lightly on her shoulders. She tenses, then—slowly—relaxes into my touch.

I knead, gentle at first, then firmer as the knots give way.

If only I had a knot. I could solve all of this for her—right here on her desk.

I keep working, fingers finding all the places she holds tension. She leans back, eyes closed, and for a minute, she looks peaceful.

She sighs, a long, shuddering breath. "That's...really nice."

Maybe there is more I can do...

I spin her chair to face me and kneel in front of her. The surprise at my audacity is etched all over her face, but I don't care. Before she can lash out at me, I say, "I know exactly what you need." I place my hands on her knees, and she almost scowls at my touch, but when I whisper, "Please, let me take care of you," her look of anger transforms to fear.

She shivers, but doesn't pull away. "Bobby, are you suggesting what I think you're suggesting?"

I nod. "Yes."

"I...I don't want things to get awkward between us," she says, voice trembling. There's a frailty in it that she rarely lets anyone see. But she lets me see it, because she trusts me.

"Too late," I joke.

She grins, just slightly, and breaks eye contact with me.

We stay like this for a while, just breathing, my hands on her thighs, touching her in a way I've never dared to before. The rest of the world fades away as I watch her face, and wait...

Finally, she says, "Okay."

CHAPTER 10
Evelyn

Bobby's hands on my thighs are the only thing holding me together. As they slide up my body, I want to make a joke about the HR department or tell him to get back to work, but my brain is too soft to form words. His touch is careful, measured—nothing like the frantic pawing I usually brace for.

The scent of him floods in. It's so warm, so comforting, that I want to bury my whole face in his shirt. I've read stories of omegas that had betas in their pack. Soothing, calming presence. That's what Bobby is.

The heat inside me is still hot and insistent, but instead of aching and angry, it feels almost satiated. Comforted. And instead of wanting a fat knot to pound me until I see stars, it wants to hug Bobby with my whole body, letting him slip into me and comfort me.

He looks up at me, like he's worshipping at the altar of me, and when his hands reach the hem of my skirt, lifting it up my thighs, I want to protest, to remind him I'm his boss, that this is a breach of a dozen policies. But I can't. The truth is, I want this. Maybe more than I've ever wanted anything.

Every inch of skin he touches sparks. And the moment my skirt is hiked high enough that a second longer our relationship will be irreparably changed, he hesitates. "Tell me if you want me to stop," he says.

I shake my head, then, emboldened, reach for him, fisting my hand in his shirt. The fabric is soft, and beneath it I can feel the steady beat of his heart. I tug, just enough to bring him closer.

He moves in, slowly, giving me a chance to change my mind. When our lips touch, it's tentative—almost chaste.

We pull back, look into each other's eyes, and take a moment to acknowledge what we have just done.

He moves in again. He kisses me like I'm something precious, something fragile. I melt into it, heat washing away every last bit of shame.

His hands still haven't moved. They remain just at my hips, grounding me. My own hands are restless, wandering up his arms, memorizing the shape of him. I'm hungry, starving, and the only thing I crave is him.

We break for air, and he looks at me like he's memorizing me, too.

I whine, needy, annoyed that he won't just fuck me already. *Why is he still hesitating?*

I try to pull him close again, but he looks to the side and says, "Let's move to the nest."

He's always thinking about my comfort.

My whole body lights up in anticipation, and I nod.

He helps me up, steadying me when my knees almost buckle.

He guides me to my nest and ensures I'm comfortable before sitting beside me. I forgot what it was like to be with someone who cared about my comfort. I haven't had that in so long.

I tried to convince myself I didn't need it. I tried to convince myself that being with someone who was rough with me, treated me like an object to fill with his seed, was what I preferred. I tried to convince myself it was empowering. That it showed I wasn't fragile. That I could handle the pain. That my withstanding it proved I was just as powerful as the three alphas pummeling me with their supposed love.

But afterward, I'd break away from the pack, tuck myself into my own corner of the bed, and hug my knees, crying and purring, trying to give myself the comfort I desperately needed and wishing I had more.

And every time, they wouldn't even notice. They'd just remain fast asleep, locked in an embrace that excluded me.

Bobby leans in and kisses me again, deeper this time, and the dam breaks. I grab him by the collar and pull him down so that he's lying on top of me. All that matters is the feel of his mouth, his hands, the warmth of his body pressed to mine.

Bobby untucks my shirt from my skirt and traces the bare skin of my midriff. Everywhere he touches feels like fire. He takes his time, exploring, learning what makes me shiver. He's always cataloged my every whim, my every need, and I suspect he's excited to have an opportunity to collect more data. When his hand finally finds my breast, I moan, shameless.

He smiles, then kisses down my neck, lingering at my pulse point. His skin is so soft and smooth, and I love it. He shifts his weight to the side, and I miss the feel of him, until I realize he's moved so his other hand can work its way up my inner thigh unburdened.

I hold my breath as his hand gets closer, and when it finally cups me through my panties, I gasp, arching into him.

He pauses, checking my face for any hint of uncertainty. When he sees none, he presses harder, rubbing slow circles that make my whole body pulse to the rhythm he sets.

"You're so wet," he murmurs, more awed than lewd.

"Yeah," I breathe, dizzy with want and wet with slick.

I guess he's never been with an omega before.

He strokes me through the fabric, patient and attentive, never rushing. When he finally slips a finger inside my panties, finger tracing the seam of my slit, so gentle, like a feather, barely even there, I nearly come undone.

It's been so long—so damn long—since anyone touched me like this.

He parts my folds and matches my moan when his fingers finally enter me. He works me, slow at first, then builds as I writhe against his hand.

I whimper, needy, and for once, I don't care. I don't feel pathetic. I want him to hear it, want him to know how badly I need this. I want him to know how badly I need him.

He slides another finger in, curling just right, and allows his thumb to find my clit. It works in small, perfect circles.

I'm shaking, sweat-damp and frantic, but he doesn't let up.

I come hard, shuddering so violently I almost slide off the couch. He holds me through it, murmuring sweet nothings in my ear, "That's it, Evelyn, just let go. Let me help you."

When I finally catch my breath, I open my eyes. He's watching me, lips parted, face flushed, waiting for my next word.

The heat within me still simmers, desperate for him to continue touching me. I want more. I want all of him.

"More?" he asks, tentative, reading my mind.

"Yes," I say, greedy.

He turns me so that I'm sitting on the couch and drops to his knees, settling between my thighs.

He kisses up my legs, inch by inch, until he's right where I want him. He hooks his fingers in my panties, tugs them down, and pauses.

I brace myself for judgment, but all I see is awe.

All restraint leaves him as he buries his face in me. He's licking and sucking like a man starved, and the only thing that can quell his hunger is my slick.

He slides his fingers inside me at the exact moment he pulls my clit into a deep, hard suck. I almost scream; the pleasure is so unbelievable.

He holds me open, feasting, taking me apart piece by piece. I grab the back of his head, grinding against his mouth, riding the wave of ecstasy that every deep thrust of my hips brings.

When I come this time, it's different—slow and blooming, like a flower opening in the sun.

I moan, "Bobby, oh, Bobby," chanting his name over and over, until it's the only word I know.

He stays there until I'm done, pushing him away, unable to receive any further pleasure.

He climbs beside me and pulls me into a hug, before cradling my head in his lap. He strokes my hair and coos at me, humming softly, until I remember how to speak.

I turn, curl into him, and pull blankets around me. For the first time in ages, I feel safe, wrapped in the warm nest he built me and comforted by his delicious cinnamon.

"Thank you," I whisper into his belly button.

He smiles, brushing a strand of hair from my face. "Anytime, boss."

I snort. "You're fired."

We laugh, and before I can sink into self-doubt, he leans down and kisses my temple—always knowing exactly what I need.

I close my eyes and realize the pain that had persistently hammered inside me has truly receded.

CHAPTER 11
Tim

My heart races as I wait for this elevator, which usually feels too fast, to take its sweet ass time zipping me to our floor. I'm not late, per se, since today is technically my day off, but I hoped to review my notes before meeting with Evelyn.

Everything hinges on this deal, and I need it to go perfectly.

Everything.

If this pitch goes well, it could be the Hail Mary we needed to meet our Q4 goals. Not only will I get a huge bonus, but the rest of the team will, as well. And since I lined up the deal, if it goes through, Evelyn promised to make me Creative Director not just of the project, but of the studio.

But the potential bonus and promotion that hinge on this deal aren't really what have me panicked. It's the fact that I've convinced myself that closing this deal will finally prove me worthy of Evelyn and will finally give me the courage to tell her how I feel. She's not packed up with those douche bags anymore, and I need to do this before she finds another set of alphas that hate me and won't let me near her except at work.

When the doors finally open, revealing our floor, I breathe a little easier. There's a scent in the air: freshly baked gingerbread cookies and a hint of what might be cinnamon.

Did the cleaners decide to swap out their usual sterile-smelling spray for something more festive?

The second I notice it, I can't stop noticing it. It's nostalgic, reminding me of something I can't quite place. Something that stirs joy and sadness and arousal. It follows me all the way to Evelyn's office.

The blinds to her glass-walled office are fully drawn, which is weird, but the door is open. When I'm finally close enough to see in, I see a small mountain of fluff where her couch usually is. It's a chaos of blankets and pillows, plus at least two stuffed animals I've never seen before. A mess of brown hair flags the top of the mountain, and one bare foot sticks out of the bottom of the heap.

Is she nesting?

That's when it hits me: she's in heat. Memories of her first heat flood my mind.

Gingerbread. I remember.

But, where is the cinnamon coming from?

I knock. Not loud, I know better if she's in heat than to make any loud or sudden noises, but just loud enough for her to hear.

She rolls over and blinks at the light I'm letting in. "Hey, Tim."

"Morning, Evie," I reply.

She struggles upright, clutching a cup of tea.

"Rough morning?" I ask.

She gives a weak half-smile. "You could say that. Ready for this pitch?"

I want to ask, "Are you?" but know that's a fast train to hell. Instead, I say, "Ready as I'll ever be. Want me to walk you through it before—?"

A door slams, hard, down the hall. I don't even need to look. Bob is here. He's the only person in the company who takes the stairs up all these flights, and he's the only person, other than me, who would insist on working on a holiday just because Evelyn is.

Bob walks into the room, more chipper than usual. His eyes are wide, and his normally well-coiffed hair is a little chaotic. He's not really one for change, so I doubt he's changed up his style. He strolls right past me, not acknowledging me, and hands Evelyn a paper bag, then dips down so she can grab a cup from a cardboard drink tray. Only after she's received her treats does he acknowledge me and provide me with a bag and a cup, as well.

"Thanks, Bob," I say, taking my usual order from him and sitting in the chair in front of Evenlyn's desk, the couch is obviously out of the question. Bob doesn't respond, simply nods and…sits next to Evelyn on her couch…her nest. My heart drops.

Did something happen between them?

She peers into her bag, and before she can ask, Bob says, "They were out of your usual, but I was able to get them to whip up something special for you."

Evelyn just stares into the bag, then at Bob. "What is this 'something special'?"

Bob beams. "They said it was a 'pre-heat' special." He pauses and blushes, looking at me, realizing he's addressing the elephant in the room.

I dare to ask, "You're in heat?"

Evelyn makes a noise that's part denial, part embarrassment. "Pre-heat."

I know she'll be annoyed, but I say it anyway, worried about her, "But…we have two alphas coming into the office today."

Bob sighs and holds up three fingers. "Three."

"What!? Evie, that's…"

Evelyn groans. "It's fine, Tim. I'm feeling much more in control now. I can handle this."

I look at my childhood friend. She's always been in denial about the effect her biology has on alphas. "That's not what I mean—"

She cuts me off, "They can handle themselves, too. We're all adults. All civilized. Plus, it's pre-heat, not actual heat. It'll be fine."

I don't think she's correct, but I won't fight her. It's her body, and it's not my place to tell her how it works.

I shrug, trying to be as nonchalant as possible. "If you say so."

"I do," she says in that way that tells me to shut the fuck up.

Bob smiles wider than I've ever seen him and asks with an inflection of pure, unbridled joy, "Do we want to run through the pitch?" I peer at him, trying to ascertain if my suspicions are correct. He's looking at

Evelyn with the goofiest smile. He always looks at her like a beta desperately in love, but...usually, he doesn't look so happy about it.

Something definitely happened between them.

Before I can spiral over that, Evelyn says, "Yeah, let's do that. Thanks again, Tim, for lining this up. If we land this, it can really pull us out of the red for the year."

She stands and straightens her hair. Bob also stands and opens her hidden closet. He pulls clothes out and begins the process of either laying them out or holding them up for her to nod at.

I watch them, studying them and noting small gestures. A slight touch here. A lingering hand there. Nothing overt, but they've obviously fucked.

I swallow hard and snap out of it when Evelyn asks, "Tim? Can you go over the pitch with us?"

"Oh, uh, sorry. Sure, yeah. The client is Chris Yore, Dr. Chris Yore, I'm sure you've heard of him."

Bob looks at me blankly, obviously having never heard of him, but Evelyn adds, "Yeah, he's a retired pro gamer, right?"

"Yeah. So, I've known Chris for quite a while. He and I play *Fated 2* together online. He uses those ex-pro-gamer reflexes to perform neurosurgery now. He's got a ton of advanced degrees."

Evelyn makes a face, indicating she's impressed, then asks, "What's the game? I want to be sure we're aligned."

I wish I had had time to run this by her before now, but Chris didn't even agree to do this until the day before yesterday. Since that moment, I've been heads down, working on this deck and trying to come up with the perfect game.

I review my notes, trying not to let my hands tremble. This is my first time leading a pitch as Creative Director. The stakes are high. If I nail it, I'll be indispensable. If I fuck it up, I might fall into another month-long depression that requires me to change careers...again.

"Okay," I say and take a breath. "It's a narrative-driven medical sim in which the player is a trauma surgeon. But instead of the usual surgery porn, the emphasis is on managing relationships with colleagues, patients, and the media. Every choice has a personal and professional cost, affecting the game's overall narrative."

Evelyn's eyes sharpen. "Okay, great. That sounds really on-brand for us. We can reuse some of the narrative engine that Elizabeth built for *Torchbearer*."

"Exactly," I say, relieved she gets it. I look at my watch, nervousness overwhelming me, but I try to conceal it. "So, uh, the client is arriving at 11:30?"

Bob nods. "Yep. Speaking of, I've got to call security and review the protocol for alphas entering the building." He stops and gives Evelyn a small smile before fully exiting the room. She sips her coffee, pretending not to smile back, but obviously does.

When he's gone, the silence that follows is almost unbearable, but I can't quite bring myself to say anything. I want to continue to run through the game with her, but right now, all I can think about is the way she was looking at Bob when he left.

Evelyn looks at me, and the slight smile on her face falls to her usual grimace when she asks, "You okay, Tim?"

No. "Absolutely."

She knows I'm lying. She just tilts her head and waits for me to confess.

So, I say, "I just wish you'd told me."

She blinks. "Told you what?"

That you were going to fuck Bob instead of asking me for help.

I want to lie again. Instead, I give the half-truth. "That you were... going into heat."

She looks away, jaw clenched. "I didn't want to make it your problem."

I swallow hard. I can't tell if she's saying she didn't want to burden me with it mentally or if she didn't want my help. "It's not a problem. Not for me." She's been my best friend since we were kids. She's always tried to hide this side of herself from me. I want to tell her that I can help her through it, like I did during her first heat, but I know how she is about getting help. And I know that we have not spoken of that week in twenty years. We pretend it never happened. It also seems like maybe she has Bob to help her now. Since two betas just equal two not-alphas, I doubt she'd appreciate my assistance, anyway.

She shakes her head, but her eyes are glassy. "I'll be fine. Once today is over, I'll take the rest of the year off. Maybe an extra week."

I nod, but I don't believe her.

She sets her cup down. "You're going to do great, you know."

"Yeah?"

"Yeah." She smiles, that smile I fucking live for. "I wouldn't have put you in charge if I didn't think you could handle it."

The praise hits me harder than I expect. My eyes sting, and I have to look away. Five years ago, I had a bit of a...let's call it a meltdown. I was a beta lawyer in an alpha world, and I just...couldn't do it anymore.

I knew next to shit about making video games, but Evelyn got me a job as a design intern, and I've been climbing my way up the ladder since. Today, she could put me at the top of it. But I have a tendency to fall the moment I get too high, unable to handle the pressure that comes with success, and she knows that about me, even if she chooses to ignore it.

"Tim. You got this. I know it. You're the only person who gets me."

And you're the only person who gets me.

We stand side by side, like nothing in the world could break us, except maybe the memory of Bob's goofy lovelorn smile.

CHAPTER 12
Chris

This whole thing started as a joke. That's what I tell myself, anyway, as I sit wedged in the back of a supposedly spacious sedan and watch the Minneapolis skyline unravel through tinted glass.

How did I let him talk me into this?

The car's filtration is state-of-the-art, designed to neutralize the strongest pheromones, but something is going on with me today. I'm keyed up and I'm not sure why.

Probably because I finally get to meet him.

I roll the window down a hair, hoping some of the winter air will cool me down, pheromones be damned. Doesn't help.

My phone buzzes right after the driver says, "That's it right there. I just need to find a safe place to pull over."

TIM RIVERA

almost here, doc?

Tim's text is short, all lowercase, as always. He's the only person I know who still texts instead of voice dictating, which makes every message feel personal and intentional. Written just for me. I thumb a reply, trying to emulate his casual style.

eta 2 min. u ready?

yep. can't wait to meet irl.

same

still on for drinks after to celebrate?

assuming you'll win me over?

this pitch is so good I have no doubt

My heart races, and I roll the window down further, triggering a look from the driver that essentially says, "fucking alphas, not everyone runs hot like you."

I smile apologetically. "So, sorry, this suit is sweltering."

"No problem, sir," he says with a voice that's polite and business-like, but still implies it probably is a problem.

We park and I fold out of the car, thanking the driver. I open my phone and leave a five-star review. I make sure to rate it favorably for rut-suppressing tech and hover my finger over the "spacious" button. I consider it. It was the perfect alpha ride. It was cramped for me, but I'm a big guy—everything is cramped for me. I click the button.

I check my appearance in my phone's camera, not unpleased, but less than enthused, and steel myself for the walk toward the building.

The building is what I expected—steel, glass, incredibly modern. It's also decked out with enough cameras and other security measures to make the state penitentiary look unguarded. The ground floor is all polished concrete and empty space.

I approach an automated kiosk, and a camera zooms in on my face. A disembodied voice says, "Welcome, Dr. Christopher Yore. Please approach the retina scanner."

Tim mentioned this. He told me security has to be extra tight because his boss is an omega. They don't keep a lot of guards on duty, since most guards are alphas, and are essentially what she needs protection from most of the time.

I scan my eye, and the kiosk says, "Identity verified. Please scan the QR code in your *SuppDose* app to verify you are up-to-date on your suppressants. A note signed by a licensed physician will also be accepted, but will need manual verification. Please expect delays of…" It pauses, performing some calculation, "one hundred fifty-seven minutes for manual verification."

Well, good thing I have the app.

I scan the QR code, and after only a few seconds, a cute little song plays. The message "Verified" with a giant green check mark and confetti displays on the screen.

Is this much fanfare really necessary?

Less than a moment later, the first in a series of glass, airlock-like doors opens to allow me entrance.

I enter the antechamber and am blocked by another glass door.

A video feed turns on above it, revealing a remote guard. He says in a gruff voice, "When you hear the countdown, please ensure all limbs are not within the red zone," without looking up. I move out of the area where the ground has been painted red, assuming it must be the red zone. I want to ask, to ensure I don't lose any limbs, but he's not on the screen anymore.

He returns and still doesn't look up. He must be annoyed to be working on a holiday.

"Sorry to have you working on a holiday, buddy," I say, flashing a smile at him, unsure if he can even hear me.

He finally looks up from whatever he was distracted by and says, voice less gruff, "Oh, wow. Chris Yore. Nice to meet you."

"You, too."

I guess he didn't read the data the kiosk collected.

A mechanical countdown starts, and the door behind me shuts slowly enough that I'm not sure why they need the whole loss-of-limbs warning. I guess it's designed to stop a rutting alpha, and we aren't the smartest of creatures in that state.

"Please proceed through the next door, Mr. Yore," the guard says as the next set of doors opens.

I consider correcting him, "Dr. Yore," but instead, I complete his request with a nod. He appears on another screen above a third glass door. We go through the same song and dance yet again.

Now I'm stopped by elevator doors with no buttons. The guard appears on a screen above them. I wait for the doors at my back to close, so painfully slow. Then the guard says, "Alright, I'll open the elevator for you and will send it right up. Happy holidays." The video feed clicks off before I can reply with my thanks and holiday salutations.

The elevator doors open, and I walk through them. They are just a little too short for me, and I have to dip my head slightly to enter a mirrored box. There are no buttons inside the elevator either. I recall the guard saying he'd send the elevator up for me, so I just step in and hope for the best.

The elevator ride is silent and too fast, but I stare at my reflection: suit perfect, tie loose, hair mussed in a way that looks unintentional, yet still dapper. I look exactly like the version of myself I'd designed for this meeting: a guy who's not uptight and definitely has gotten laid within the last few years. Neither are true, but at least I accomplished the look, which is both comforting and a little depressing.

I need to impress Tim. I cannot spend another Christmas alone.

I've had a crush on Tim for years, even though I've never met him in person. We stay up late gaming together and talking about everything. The first time we got on a video call, I was rendered speechless by how fucking handsome he was. I've been putty in his hands ever since, not that I think he's aware.

The other night, he vented to me about work as we did a loot rush together. He told me the company had not met its quarterly goals and that he desperately hoped to be promoted from Lead Designer to Creative Director. I jokingly said I'd hire him to make a game, and like many people when I joke, he didn't realize I was joking. Instead of disappointing him, I decided to go for it. I'm playing hard to get, but honestly, at this point, he could pitch me the biggest load of crap game concept ever conceived and I'd fund it, just to see him smile.

Thank God I can afford it.

I don't know if he's interested in men, but I'm hoping this will give me the opportunity to find out. I've tried to ask him multiple times, but have always wussed out: real alpha of me, I know.

We plan to get drinks after, and that's when I hope to shoot my shot. I've got my hotel room all prepped and ready to go, just in case he decides to come back to it with me tonight. This would obviously be the best-case scenario. It's been so fucking long since I've gotten laid. But I'd settle for just having drinks with a friend and not spending Christmas Eve alone.

This time of year always makes me...lonely...horny. It always makes me think of her: the one that got away. Maybe this will be an opportunity to finally move on.

When the elevator stops and the doors open, I'm greeted by the familiar scent of gingerbread. I'd recognize it anywhere, since it's haunted me for the last twenty years. It's strong, sweet, and almost edible. I try to ignore it and walk into the reception area.

It's empty, save for a bowl of individually wrapped hard candies and a touchscreen directory that immediately pings my name: "Welcome, Dr. Yore."

I stand, unsure where to go when a door opens and out strolls the tallest, most handsome beta I've ever seen.

Tim.

He's fucking beautiful. More perfect than I could have hoped for. He's got the body of an alpha but the posture of a beta, careful, on the verge of apologizing for being in your way.

And, fuck, he smells like spiced cranberries.

Tim crosses to me, hand out to shake mine. "Chris," he says. "Great to finally meet you in person." His voice is low, a little hesitant, with that Midwestern vowel stretch that always makes me swoon on game chat.

I'm surprised by how tall he is. On video, you lose the scale. The way his shoulders took up space indicated he was large for a beta, but not this large. "Likewise, Tiny Tim." I can't help the grin. The gamer tag is obviously a joke. He wouldn't be considered tiny to most people, except maybe me. At 7 feet tall, most people are short to me. But Tim has to be at least 6'4".

I quicken my step to meet his hand. When we shake, tiny sparkles of joy practically shoot from my fingers. His grip is stronger than I expected. I hold his hand a little longer than I should, and must give him that "the big man wants to fuck you look," because he flushes a little.

With his hand returned to him, he says, "Thanks so much for coming out here, man. This means so much to me."

"Of course...man," I say, trying to emulate his vernacular.

"This way. We're headed to Conference Room C."

He walks through the door he just came through, and when I bend to do the same, he laughs. "Gosh, that must suck, having to duck at every doorway."

It's that kind of observation that draws me to him. I've always felt like I couldn't complain about my height, because everyone acts like it's such a blessing. But, for me, it's as much of a curse as being the runt of my litter was as a kid. "Yeah, it kind of does." I laugh.

I follow him through a maze of glass and brushed metal. The office is deserted, lights on but no humans in sight. I guess it's a holiday for most of the team.

Good. Less chance of being recognized.

As we walk, he points out cool architectural features of the building and stops at various game memorabilia, telling me little stories about how he worked on the games.

At the far end of the office suite, a conference room door is open, and I can hear voices within as we approach. The first voice is muffled, but there's a power to it, a kind of effortless command, despite its feminine song. The second is softer, gentler, kinder, and deeper.

I repress the urge to fidget and try to maintain my jovial smile as Tim continues to tell me about his work. I'm eating up every word he says, trying to be as chill as possible, but my heart is racing more than it should.

I know it's been a long time since I've gotten laid. I know it's been a long time since I've met with anyone outside of work. And I know this spontaneous meeting with Tim is kind of a big deal for me, but I'm not sure why he's having such an effect on me.

It's gotta be his pheromones. His spiced cranberries, paired with whatever that gingerbread scent is, are just too much like her: that gorgeous omega with the fox scarf that has held my heart for twenty years. The reason I've stayed single all these years. I shake my head and tell the Proust Effect to go fuck itself. I can't let it consume me. I need to move on.

After the mini tour of "all things Tim," we finally arrive at the open conference room door. He strolls in, and I follow. The room is big enough for twenty, but only two seats are occupied.

They both turn, and my heart, which was racing, officially stops.

My mouth hangs agape when Tim says, "Dr. Chris Yore, this is Evelyn Charles, CEO. And Bob Andrews, admin lead."

If Tim's attractiveness hit me like a truck, seeing these other two hits me like a freight train.

Evelyn stands and walks toward me, hand outstretched. "Dr. Yore," she says.

But I can barely muster a response.

The smell of gingerbread overwhelms me.

It's her.

I sputter, "Call me Chris, please," and swallow hard.

Her handshake is quick and dry, but the moment our hands touch, reality loses focus for me.

It's her.

I've found her.

I glance at Tim.

It's him. That's why he smelled familiar.

I can't believe I've found them—after all this time.

Bob approaches me, and I feel like I'm in a hazy dream. He's already smiling. He smells like cinnamon, and when he shakes my hand, I have to resist the urge to lick it, just to see if it matches.

They smell like Christmas.

This...this is my pack.

CHAPTER 13
Chris

They all sit, and I do the same, in a daze. My head is spinning.

What do I say? Do I tell them now or should I court them first?

It would be rude not to let Tim give me his pitch.

Tim launches into the presentation without preamble, and for the first five minutes, I do my best to tune out everything but his words. But by the second slide, my cock is fully hard, which is mortifying. Luckily, I'm positioned at the table in such a way that no one can see, but I try to hide it by crossing my legs anyway. My knee bumps the table, drawing everyone's attention to me, and now I'm suddenly aware of how much space I take up.

I want to be respectful and hear this pitch. I want to treat this with the professionalism it deserves. I came in knowing I'd probably just agree to whatever he pitched to me, overwhelmed by puppylove and lust. But I want to at least try to act as if I will be deciding with something other than my dick. Plus, I really want to see if he's as good as I suspect he is.

But the scent. It's everywhere, warping the air, making the room shimmer around the edges. It's not just one note, it's a symphony: Evelyn's gingerbread, Bob's cinnamon, and Tim's spiced cranberries.

Separate, they're powerful. Combined, they make my whole body tighten.

I know I'm up-to-date on my rut suppressants. I just verified it downstairs. But I check my phone anyway.

I don't understand what's going on here. This should not be hitting me this hard.

I grip my knee under the table and focus on the pitch: emotional realism with consequences that ripple through every part of the game's narrative. I can't believe he put this whole thing together in such a short amount of time. I like it.

I like Tim. I like him a lot.

I need him.

I need all of them.

I need to pay attention.

I like Tim's passion. It's endearing the way he stumbles over his own excitement and then doubles down, refusing to let anyone see the insecurity underneath. He's opened up to me about his anxieties. So, I know, right now, he's got one hundred worst-case scenarios running through his head about how I'm reacting. So I need to control my face as much as possible. I don't want to send mixed signals.

I smile and nod, trying to show that I am listening. I am...mostly. But I'm not able to put as much brainpower into making sure my smile isn't a sneer as I usually am.

I grin bigger, and a flash of horror crosses Tim's face. *Fuck*. When you're a big guy like me, you have to constantly be aware of how you're perceived. The whole world is terrified of you. I've spent many years perfecting my "friendliness appearance," but it's a song and dance that doesn't come naturally to me. And right now, I have no pitch and two left feet.

Evelyn politely interrupts Tim to clarify a point about the potential timeline. When she speaks, I watch how the muscles around her mouth form words, and each breath she takes causes a rise and fall of her breasts. I lean over slightly so I can see how her ass cradles in the seat. I catch myself and straighten up. I shake my head, trying to regain my wits.

I only catch the tail end of her question, but Tim handles it by referencing two studies and a user poll from last quarter. The teamwork is beautiful. I can tell they respect each other. I'm so impressed my dick gets even harder, which I didn't think was possible.

I bet they fuck well as a team, too.

Get a fucking grip, Chris.

I grip the edge of the table and plant my feet firmly on the ground, trying to ground myself and regain control of my body.

Bob hasn't said a word throughout the entire presentation. He just watches patiently, taking notes. He glances at me occasionally in a way that tells me he's the observational type. He's cataloging my reactions for later analysis. When he catches me looking at him, he gives me a slight smile.

Mine.

Mine.

Mine.

Stop it. Take a deep breath.

Bad idea...

The pheromones are getting stronger, and before I thought I was hallucinating, but now I know I can definitely see them. Swirling, sparkling, iridescent vapor in the air that I can see, touch, taste, not just smell. I can feel their scent envelop my body, embracing me in a gentle hug, tickling my balls, and tugging at my heart.

Tim shifts his stance so I can see a chart explaining how the narrative structure will work. He makes a joke and everyone laughs. I laugh, too, because I know I'm supposed to, but I don't know what I'm laughing at.

They all look at me, horrified.

Fuck. Did I laugh too loud?

I want to bury my face in the crook of Tim's neck, inhale until my lungs collapse.

I want to know what Evelyn tastes like.

I want to know what Bob sounds like when he's delirious with lust and begging for more with my knot buried deep in his mouth.

I want to know what it feels like to sink my teeth into each of their necks and how it feels when the bond link explodes out of them and crashes into me.

I need to chill.

I'm a grown fucking man. I can control myself. I have four fucking advanced degrees. I'm a god damn brain surgeon.

I force myself to look away from them and their mesmerizing scents. I pretend to take notes. But I can't.

Bob looks at me again, but this time, he doesn't look away. Instead, he smiles, slow and deliberate. It's like he's daring me to do something. Like he knows what's on my mind. Like he can tell I'm thinking about his lips wrapped around my cock. Like...he wants me to come to him.

No. That can't be true. I'm imagining that.

He makes a note on his tablet. Probably alerting security, "Client displaying classic rut behavior. Bring the tasers and the XXXL tranquilizers."

I can't stop thinking about rutting into all three of them.

I can't stop thinking about what our life will be like, spending Christmases together. I'll make them waffles with whipped cream and strawberries. Tim will get whipped cream on his nose. It'll be so cute, I'll cry. Bob and Evelyn will probably have matching pajamas. I'll give them figurines I carved from the branches of a tree I planted on the day of our bonding ceremony. We'll make love by the fire, then lie together, reading classic literature while we bask in the afterglow of our multiple orgasms and I'm knot-locked to Evelyn, putting tons of babies in her.

Oh, my fucking God, the litter of pups I'm going to put in Evelyn. How cute they'll be running around the Christmas tree.

They're all so fucking hot and all so fucking adorable. I want to hug them and protect them and murder anyone who ever makes any of them feel anything less than pure happiness.

I feel like I already know them. Everything they do feels so perfect, so familiar, so safe. It's in the way Tim fidgets with his laser pointer, the way Evelyn bites her lower lip and rolls her thumb over her pen, the way Bob's foot bounces under the table. Each action is perfectly synced to my own pulse—like we're already linked somehow.

Tim moves to a slide that breaks down the budget. He provides multiple options with various team sizes and timelines. It's a little more than I expected, but less than I have.

Take it all. Take all my money.

Take all of me.

Can betas take knots? I've never put my knot in anyone before.

Evelyn can take it. She was built for it.

I bet she gets so fucking wet.

I shift uncomfortably in my chair—a chair that I'm suddenly aware is way too small for me. I wipe my palms on my thighs and try to remember how to breathe.

The chair squeaks against the floor, turning Bob and Evelyn's attention to me. Tim is still talking, looking at his slides with his back to me.

Evelyn's eyes are on me, and her scent flares. Bob must notice because he looks at her. The fact he can tell proves we're meant to be—all of us.

It proves she wants me.

I've never had an omega want me. She's such a tiny little thing.

Will I split her in half? Nah, she can take it.

I'll have Tim and Bob prep her for me, though. I don't want to hurt her, and I'll enjoy watching them slide their dicks into her.

I look at Tim's large frame. His back is turned toward me, and his muscles are undulating through his shirt.

I wonder if Tim can take me.

My skin tingles, scalp to toes.

I'm losing my grip on reality and struggling to maintain my composure. I've never felt like this before.

I can't keep this up. I need to say something.

CHAPTER 14
Tim

I've always considered myself a personable guy. I'm pretty good at commanding attention, wowing people, getting them to laugh, getting them to buy what I'm selling, if you will. When I turn it on, it's on. Afterward, I feel like I got hit by a freight train, and I tend to ruminate over every mistake, but that's beside the point. The point is, I can turn it on and get it done.

But right now, every single trick I pull out of my sleeve is falling flat on the floor. *Limp. Pathetic.*

I don't know where I fucked up.

At first, I thought I had him. He was nodding and smiling and really seemed to be vibing with the pitch.

But around slide four, Chris's eyes glazed over, and I've been floundering since.

Perhaps I fucked up before the pitch even started. He's always been kind of an intense dude; he's an alpha, it comes with a territory. And I was getting the impression he was into me. He was all smiles and barely repressed nervous energy. After the blow I received earlier (aka realizing Bob fucked Evelyn), it was nice to feel wanted. I was going to land this pitch and then, tonight, find out if he's a pitcher or a catcher.

I'm a switch hitter, not that it matters now.

But maybe what I was reading as attraction was actually revulsion. Maybe the smiles were painted on. I showed him around the office and tried to wow him with my best stories. But by the end of the tour, every reaction was slightly delayed, as if he were trying to be polite. I thought it was nervousness...but...

Maybe I annoyed him?

Maybe I was being too much.

Maybe I gave him the ick.

By slide five, he was just staring at the table in front of him, not looking at me or my slides, grinding his teeth and gripping the edge of the table like it was a life raft and he was out to sea.

And it went downhill from there. With every word I uttered, he grimaced further, as if everything I said was the worst thing any person had ever said. Every time I glanced over, his jaw was working so hard I was afraid he'd shatter his own teeth.

I stopped looking and tried to power through. I kept talking, because that's what you do when you're losing: you try to brute-force your way through it. I pulled out all the stops—all the jokes. Evelyn even popped in to set me up, ask me a question that let me show how much research is behind what I'm pitching, but...nothing...

And now, I'm at the end of the pitch, discussing potential budgets and timelines, and I'm not even sure what the point is. Chris is thoroughly checked out. His eyes are fucking closed, and he appears to be holding his breath.

Maybe I'm misreading him. Maybe it's because I'm still recuperating from the psychological damage of Bob and Evelyn fucking. Maybe I'm being overly sensitive—I tend to be.

I'll make a joke about it. Lighten the air. See how he reacts. "Looks like I'm putting Chris to sleep."

Chris opens his eyes, and I swear he's not seeing me at all. His gaze slides off my face and lands somewhere over my right shoulder. I try to make eye contact, but he's unreachable, like someone's swapped him out for a cardboard cutout. I balk, unable to continue talking.

Should I just confront him? Ask him what the fuck is up?

Evelyn and Bob are looking at him, too, and I can tell they're also trying to decide what to do.

I open my mouth, but nothing comes out. My brain locks up, unable to make a choice.

Suddenly, Chris pushes himself upright. He stands so abruptly that the chair skids back and slams into the wall with a sound like a gunshot.

We all jump.

He looks at Evelyn, then Bob, then at me. He swallows, then says in a low, measured tone, as if it takes all his energy to say each word: "I'm sorry, Tim. I can't listen to any more of this pitch."

The words hit like a physical blow. I feel my vision tunnel in, black at the edges.

CHAPTER 15

I'm not the type of man who enjoys losing control.

Precision, planning, patterns, and predictability: that's my safe zone.

So when I realized I had blacked out in the middle of Tim's pitch, the best I could do was bite the inside of my cheek, try to remember the last thing anyone said, and pray to every obsolete god that Tim would forgive me for stopping him.

Now I'm standing here, ashamed, after having made a bit of a spectacle of myself.

Tim looks like I just snapped his spinal cord, disconnecting his brain from the rest of his body. His face is pale, his mouth slightly open, and sweat is clumping his hair around his face. This was so important to him, and I've thoroughly fucked it up.

He composes himself just long enough to place his laser pointer on the table and whisper to Evelyn, "I'll be at my desk." He heads for the door, but I block it, thankful for my size in this moment. He looks like he might punch me, betrayal etched all over his face, but obviously thinks better of it.

I manage to say, "I'm sorry, Tim. Please, stay. Let me explain."

Evelyn stands and moves to place herself between me and Tim. It's such a non-omega move, I'm taken aback by it. It's protective and...

fucking hot. She puts her hand on Tim's shoulder, locking eyes with him and conveying some message without words—the kind of message only two people who know each other very well can convey. Jealousy floods me, and the scent of pine spills out of me, mixing beautifully with theirs.

They all notice. Tim and Bob only slightly—you can see it in the way their pupils dilate and their nostrils flare—but the fact that they notice at all proves I'm right about them being my pack. But Evelyn really notices. Her body almost launches itself toward me, but she stops herself. I've never perfumed near an omega before, and her reaction, no matter how much she controls it, makes me want to use myself as a human shield against anything that might come her way. If I could melt my body down to its base components, pour it into a suit of armor mold, and wrap myself around this woman, I would.

She scowls at me, anger contorting her beautiful, delicate face, and squares up against me, which is weirdly terrifying even though I probably outweigh her by about two hundred pounds and tower two feet above her.

Her eyes narrow. "Are you rutting?" she demands, which is a valid question given I just sprayed my pine all over the room.

I let out a slight nervous laugh. "No. I mean, maybe a little. But not like that. It's—" I stop, unsure how to phrase it. "I changed my suppressant patch at five this morning," I offer, tapping at my leg, where the patch is stuck, seeping continuous pharmaceuticals into my bloodstream. "It's slow release."

Her chin tips up, defiant. "Then pull yourself together."

The words hit me right in the solar plexus. For a second, I feel like a kid again, the smallest alpha in a family of giants, trying to hide how much I craved structure and approval. I almost say, "Yes, ma'am," but I just nod instead.

I deserved that. I should be more in control of this.

Tim towers behind her, head hung, looking like he wants to run and hide. She brushes his arm, reassuringly, and says way more gently than she just spoke to me, "Sit, Tim. Let's retro this, okay?"

He also just nods, then walks to the other side of the table to sit next to Bob, whose eyes are wide in bewilderment.

Evelyn steels herself, brushes invisible lint off her suit jacket, crosses her arms, and cocks her head. She looks me up and down, and if I couldn't smell the lust coming off of her, I'd be fooled by the charade. "Was it something we did? Was there a problem with the deck? The pitch? We can change it. We just need to know what went wrong."

I notice that she says, "We," not "Tim," and I am in awe of the leadership. She isn't throwing him under the bus; she isn't blaming him; she's taking this on with him as a team.

God, I love this woman.

I half expect her to say, "Well?" when I take another moment to compose myself.

I look at Tim and plead with him, "Nothing went wrong. The pitch was great. I'm just...having trouble listening to it." I realize how that sounds, and I try to correct: "I'm sorry, my brain is just...addled. It's... it's the scent."

Evelyn turns, frowning. "I apologize. I am in pre-heat," she says, and I can tell she hates the admission. But then she adds, "However, I would think an alpha of your educational background could handle a single omega in pre-heat, especially with a supposed slow-release suppressant patch stuck to your leg."

That one cut to the core.

"It's...it's not just you." I swallow hard. The sound is wet and loud. My tongue feels thick, useless. "It's all of you. You're my pack."

She scrunches her nose at me, glaring, arms still folded, incredulity marring her pretty face. I want to boop her nose and hug her, but I'm afraid she'd scratch my eyes out.

Tim and Bob, on the other hand, exchange a look that implies I just put words to something they've known all along, hidden deep within their psyche; they just needed someone to unlock it for them.

She scoffs. "And what? Just because you say so, I'm supposed to what? Get on my knees and let you claim me?"

I mean, honestly, I was kinda hoping you would, yeah.

"Can't you tell? You...you all smell like Christmas," I say, reaching forward, wanting to embrace her.

She backs away, avoiding my touch and sneering. "Oh, and because you smell like a Christmas tree, I'm supposed to swoon?" *Aww, she thinks I smell like a Christmas tree.* "Well, unfortunately for you, I hate Christmas." She walks to where she had been seated and begins to gather her things. "I think we should all agree that this business relationship will not be moving forward. Good day, Dr. Yore. Bob, will you please see him out?"

Bob doesn't move. He and Tim just stare at me with that look people get when they've found their scent-matched pack mate. I return the look because I can't be rude to my precious packmates.

My packmates.

While Bob and Tim are on my side, Evelyn is obviously not. She's had enough of me and looks like she will heave me out of the room herself.

I'd honestly love to see her try. At least then she'd be touching me.

She's gathered her things and is now looking at Bob like he's lost his damn mind. "Bobby?" she asks, the anger in her voice now replaced with confusion.

"I think he's right," Bob says, meekly. Tim nods, and then the smile he had earlier finally returns to his face.

I'm so elated that I begin to walk toward them, ready to embrace them, but I'm stopped dead in my tracks when Evelyn nearly spits, "Bullshit."

She is seething with rage, and her corporate composure is slipping.

I ask her, "Why do you hate Christmas? Is it because of your first heat?"

Her attention whips toward me, and she glares.

I exhale slowly and decide just to say it. "I recognized you. Your scent. Both of your scents," I say, gesturing between her and Tim. I focus on a fixed point above her head so I can finish the sentence. "From a tournament. Christmas Eve. Twenty years ago. You wore a scarf with little foxes on it. You dominated the match, then—" I stop, not wanting to bring up the rest.

Evelyn doesn't react for a heartbeat. Then: "Yes, that was me."

"I knew it. I'd never forget that gingerbread. Until today, I thought it was gingerbread and spiced cranberries, though," I say, blushing and glancing at Tim. He shifts in his chair and scowls. I'm not sure why. "I didn't realize the spiced cranberries was the beta that was with you.

Memory is a funny thing." I laugh, trying to diffuse the situation, because for some reason, Tim seems incredibly pissed at me again.

Bob looks between the three of us, his eyes finally landing on Evelyn. "What is he talking about?" he asks her.

She shrugs, but I can tell she's thrown. "I went into my first heat very suddenly. At a video game tournament filled with nerdy alphas. They all went into a rut."

There's a beat. I try to say something reassuring, but all that comes out is, "I've been looking for you since that day."

Bob's eyebrows go up. "Wait. Did you...Did you attack her?"

Oh, God. Evelyn and Tim probably think I was one of those alphas who went into a rut, too.

"No! No! I helped her. I kept it together and helped her out. I fought them off. Then a beta, Tim, came for her..."

I don't mention that I went into a rut almost immediately after I knew she was safe.

Evelyn circles the table, coming within arm's reach. She looks me up and down, studying me, trying to judge the validity of my claim. "The alpha that saved me was the smallest one in the room."

"I grew," I say. "A lot."

CHAPTER 16
Evelyn

There's no way this giant of a man is that little alpha who helped me on that fateful Christmas Eve twenty years ago.

I was a senior in high school, and Tim had dared me to enter the *Embrace the Suck* tournament. I knew I was good at the game, but I didn't think I was good enough to enter a tournament. But after multiple overtime rounds and a total of nineteen grueling hours, I won.

It was the happiest moment of my life.

Until it wasn't.

The moment my hands wrapped around the trophy, a deep, searing pain burned through me. I fell to the ground, doubled over in pain, screaming, not understanding what was going on with me.

I was eighteen: too old to be going through my first heat. I thought I had dodged that bullet; I was lucky I wouldn't have to deal with the curse my father dealt with. But there I was, on the ground, writhing in pain, being proven wrong.

The lust hadn't even kicked in by the time my opponents started rutting. What began as a bunch of sneering, mean, misogynist gamers turned into a bunch of potential rapists, hyped up on energy drinks—mad that they were beaten not only by a girl, but an omega girl.

Then, a tiny knight in shining braces came to my rescue. An alpha so small it was hard to believe he was one. He held his second-place trophy like a baseball bat, standing in front of me, ready to murder them all, intervening with precisely the amount of violence needed. They were all at least twice his size, but it didn't matter—he stood his ground. "Don't fucking touch her!" he squeaked, his voice cracking. Tim rushed me out, just as the boy cracked an assailant over the head.

Tim ran nearly every red light on the way to my house. The terror on his face increased with each painful scream I let out, but despite his panic, he did exactly what I needed him to: he got me to my nest. The problem was that my nest was being converted into a home gym. When I turned eighteen and showed no signs of omeganess, we all assumed I was a beta.

When Tim got me to my nest/home gym, he couldn't just leave me there. It wasn't safe. So he stayed and took care of me. I don't recall most of it, as I was delirious with pain and lust, but I do remember that was the last time in my life I felt truly cared for.

Afterward, we did the thing teenagers tend to do: not talk about it. We pretended it never happened, but I secretly hoped we'd take our relationship to the next level. I waited too long to talk about it with him, though. He went off to college shortly after to become a lawyer, and I... well, I tried my best to embrace the suck of being an omega. I never played that fucking game again, though. And, I've hated Christmas ever since.

As the memories flood me, I think maybe I do recall a slight scent of pine. I still don't believe this man could be that tiny alpha who saved me, but...maybe...that's why the smell of pine has always felt so safe. So stabilizing.

My sneer must relax, because Chris seems to think this is the moment he should start talking again. "I knew that day you were my mate. I looked for you for years. I didn't know your name; I only knew your gamer tag: FoxyWig. I went pro—looking for you. I got so fucking good at that game—looking for you. Then...I got good at them all—looking for you. But you were never there. I never saw you at another tournament. I never saw your gamer tag anywhere. You disappeared."

His words tug at my heartstrings. Did he really go pro just trying to find me? I don't know what to say, so I just explain why he never saw me again: "I stopped playing after that day."

"That's a shame. You were really good."

"Yeah, well...bad memories."

"Understandable."

I look at him and consider reaching out to touch him. He's huge and hot, and there is something that feels...safe. But I don't exactly have the best track record when it comes to trusting alphas.

Chris pulls his phone out of his jacket pocket. "I...know you don't believe me. But I can prove it was me." He taps away at his phone, then hands it to me. "That's me, right around that time," he says, pointing to the screen. It's a picture of a tiny alpha in the middle of a large family of large alphas. He's getting a noogie from what appears to be an older sibling. "This is the day I got my braces off." He laughs.

Tim and Bobby appear at my side, curiosity obviously calling them over. They peer down at the phone with me.

The boy who probably saved my life. It's him.

My eyes begin to water, overcome with love for that little boy. I look at the man in front of me, and I think maybe I see a resemblance.

"May I?" Chris asks, so gentle, and gestures at his phone.

I nod, unable to speak.

A tear drops on the phone. I'm not sure why, but an extreme sadness begins to overwhelm me. Two hands rub up my back, soothing me: Tim and Bobby.

Chris taps on the phone, navigating through pictures of flowers, cats, and what look like lecture notes; no people, though. Then he opens a picture with two cats, snuggling by a fire. They're super cute, and I'm confused why he's showing me this.

Then I notice it, atop the fireplace, in two pieces and dented: his trophy.

Tim appears as stunned as I am.

"It is you," I say, my voice cracking slightly. "You...you did grow."

Chris looks up from the phone and meets my eyes, caught between hope and panic. He laughs, "Yeah."

"Yeah." I pause, then—because I don't want to undersell it—"You basically saved my life that day."

He shakes his head, embarrassed. “It wasn’t a big deal.”

He’s so humble. He’s so…unalpha.

I’m sorta unomega, so…

“It was to me,” I say, and I mean it.

“And me,” Tim says, and I know he means it, too.

There’s a charge in the air, and Chris’s scent hits me again, harder this time: Pine, cold winter, ozone. “Christmas tree,” I laugh, when I realize he’s as big as one, too.

Chris says, “I’ve looked for you for so long. I can’t believe I finally found you.” The words burn through every last shield I have. He reaches out, and this time I let him touch me. He brushes the tear from my cheek, and it’s so gentle, I can’t believe this giant man is capable of it.

CHAPTER 17
Evelyn

And just like always, whenever things start going great for me, being an omega fucks shit up.

A cramp blooms in my core. It starts as a slow coil under my belly button, then snaps tight, so fast and mean I double over.

The cramps gnawed away at me for all of Tim's pitch, but I thought the orgasms Bobby gave me were sufficient to keep them from getting too bad. Apparently, I was wrong.

I have to hold on to Tim to keep from falling over. My knees lock, then tremble. Every cell in my body reroutes its energy to my core. The hair on my arms stands on end, and I'm so aware of every square inch of my skin that I want to peel it off.

Tim is still processing what is happening when Bobby reacts. Bobby's palm flattens on my lower back. "Breathe," he says, so soft in my ear it would tickle if everything didn't hurt.

Tim holds me upright, the confusion on his face now replaced with understanding and concern. His hand, not wrapped around my arm, joins Bobby's at my back. "After it passes, let's sit her down," Tim says to Bobby.

Chris just watches like an alpha in the headlights.

The cramp lets go. I suck in a breath, then another. I don't even have to tell Tim and Bobby the cramp has subsided; they just know and shuffle me to the nearest chair.

I'm shaking, and I hate that they can all see it, but the next wave is already building, this time radiating from my hips and spreading outward, white-hot and impossible to contain.

I want to scream. I want to run. But all I can do is grit my teeth and ride it out.

Bobby materializes a water bottle into my hand.

I close my eyes and drink because it gives me something to do, and the cold makes it a little easier to deal with.

Fuck my life.

I open my eyes, and Chris is on his knees in front of me, head cocked just a little as he considers me. His scent is a forcefield now, warping the air around him and making me dizzier than I already was. But it's a different kind of dizziness. It's hard to explain, but it feels... kind of like my nest.

His hands reach out to touch me, but he wavers, reconsiders, closes his eyes, and emits a soft purr instead.

The sound short-circuits my brain. My whole body locks up, then melts, then locks again. The pain subsides, then returns, then subsides again. It's almost like the pain is distracted by the sound just as much as I am.

The sweat that was beading on my hairline chills and evaporates. The heat that had burned in my core ripples down the back of my thighs, tensing their muscles and opening my legs. My skirt rides up as my thighs spread wide.

The heat and pain, once concentrated on my core, hit every cubic inch of my body, and it's so overwhelming I think I may pass out. But, suddenly, it subsides. It doesn't hurt. Not even a little. The warmth isn't even uncomfortable; it feels like a full-body hug.

Is it because he purred for me?

I realize an alpha has never purred for me before. I would focus on that. I would get really mad about what shitty packmates Jacob, Mark, and Lee were, but I'm too relaxed to give a fuck right now.

All the tension in my body releases. My head lolls back on the high-back chair, and I sigh, the sensation so soothing.

This feels...nice...

I'm not in control, though. The pain is now replaced by an overpowering lust. My legs and arms are spread wide, and I'm ready for anything that wants to insert itself into me to do so.

Bobby squeezes my shoulder, steady. "You okay?"

Yes, I'm great. You can fuck me now. Thanks.

Wait. No, I'm fucking not.

I regain control of my body and let my head fall forward, hair curtaining my face, hiding my shame. I snap my legs shut.

I'm so embarrassed.

"I'm fine," I mumble, but it's a lie so transparent I almost choke on it. "I just...need a minute to compose myself."

I can do this. I can do this.

Chris moves back. He stays at eye level with me, but he is giving me some space. "You don't have to fight it," he says, voice gentle. "No one here is going to judge you."

I want to tell him to fuck off, but I don't. I can't.

Tim kneels beside me, "You need to drink," he says, and there's a weight in his voice that makes it more command than suggestion.

Bobby places the water bottle I didn't realize I dropped back in my hand.

I nod, gulp the water, and hope the cold will cool me from the inside out.

It doesn't.

The next cramp is building, deeper this time, a pressure that pushes against every boundary I've set for myself. My vision edges with black. My legs spread, involuntarily, and my skirt hikes up another inch. I want to close them, but I can't. I'm frozen, pinned to the seat by chemistry and shame and need.

Oh my fucking God, I need them. I need all three of their dicks inserted in me. NOW.

This time, when the spasm hits, I don't try to hide it. I moan, low and guttural. Bobby and Tim's hands steady me, ground me, hold me together. And when I fall apart, they put me back together. They rub deep, slow circles on my lower back, easing the pain. With their free hands, they pet my hair, my arms, my legs.

"Shhhhh," Bobby whispers.

As the cramp subsides, I exhale, loud and guttural. And, as if I've unlodged something blocking my glands, my scent plumes out of me, so strong, so thick, Bobby and Tim shake their heads in a daze as it hits them in the face full force.

Chris's eyes go dark, hungry, but he doesn't move. He just watches, jaw flexing, every muscle in his arms cabled with restraint.

The sound he makes—half growl, half purr—wraps around me like a weighted blanket.

Tim and Bobby both lean slightly closer. And when their necks enter my periphery, spiced cranberries and cinnamon rush down my nose, coating my tongue. I can taste it. I can taste them. And all I can think about right now is taking their dicks into my mouth and sucking the seed right out of them. *It'll be so fucking delicious. A festive feast.*

Their pulse throbs in their jugulars, and I can literally see the scent secreting from their bodies in delicious, sparkly, indecent waves. It's pumping from them, every heartbeat pushing just a little more of it out, hitting my face in waves. I lick the air and almost hit Tim's jaw with my tongue.

I want to taste them.

Their scent swirls in the air, mixing with Chris's Christmas tree. And, for the first time ever, I can see my own scent, too. It blends with theirs, effortlessly.

Our scents dance together, mixing. It's like they were meant to be together. It's as if they have minds of their own and have decided that the four of us should be one unit. As if they have decided to form a pack, even if the humans who are secreting them haven't made a decision yet.

It's so beautiful.

"You got this, Evie," Tim says, then asks, "What do you need?"

The words lodge in my throat.

Nothing.

Everything.

Knot.

My eyes drift to Chris. He's as far away from me as the room will allow, fighting his own battle of control, hands fisted at his side, jaw locked tight. "You," I say, so raspy, so quiet, I'm surprised he can hear it.

He's across the room before I can blink, moving with a fluid grace that's almost inhuman. He doesn't touch me, he kneels before me, and grips the arms of my chair, caging me. He leans in, hovering about a foot from my neck and inhales, loud, low, rumbling with a purr that vibrates not just the air this time, but my whole fucking body.

His scent floods my nose and overrides every other input. I shiver as the vibrations peak my nipples and send all the blood straight to my pussy. My clit hardens, begging to be pressed. My labia swell painfully, begging someone to pound against them and relieve the pressure.

Bobby and Tim moan in unison, and their eyes close. Their heads drop and their foreheads rest on my shoulders.

Chris leans in closer, close enough that I can feel the brush of his breath on my ear. "Do you want me to stop?" he asks, voice low.

I shake my head.

He doesn't hesitate. He grips my hips and pulls me against his chest, not quite lifting me from the chair. He wraps his arms around my back and cradles my head. His grip is gentle, but there's no mistaking the strength in it.

I melt, the last of my defenses, the last of my strength gone.

The next spasm is so intense it rips a cry out of me. My body, which had just been completely limp, is now so tight I feel like I'd shatter if he lets go.

Chris purrs louder, pulling me tighter to him. Now it's not just my chest and head against his body, but my pussy is now planted firmly against his abdomen.

I arch, instinct taking over. My head falls back, and for a second I'm weightless, floating on the pulse of my own need. My body goes boneless, and I have no control over my limbs. I'm limp, featherlight, a rag doll.

I feel like I should be falling. Falling to the earth, letting it swallow me.

But Chris doesn't let me; he holds me, unyielding.

And Bobby and Tim's hands are there, steady, safe, reassuring, letting me know I can let go. None of them will let me fall.

It's as if these three are the only things stopping gravity from pulling my body straight down to the pits of hell.

I almost lose consciousness as the pain takes me.

When the spasm fades, they're all still there: Chris's arms are still around me, heartbeat thudding against my chest, purr vibrating the air around me; Bobby is smoothing my hair, pressing a water bottle against my lips; and Tim is nuzzling my shoulder, whispering, reassuring, praising.

For the first time in years, I don't feel alone.

I feel protected. I feel safe. I feel cared for.

I'm not a thing to be taken advantage of. I'm someone to love, to cherish, to protect.

I close my eyes and let myself rest, just for a moment.

CHAPTER 18
Tim

We're all kneeling beside her, caressing her, calming her, helping her through the pain. The world around me has dulled, and the only thing I can see is the three of them. The only thing I can feel is them. It's like we're all on a video call with our background blur filters on.

I can smell it: the cinnamon, the gingerbread, the fresh morning snow and pine. And, it does smell like Christmas. It gives me that same feeling I had when I was a kid on Christmas morning: excited, hopeful, safe, loved. Like it's going to be the best fucking day ever. It's a feeling I forgot.

Chris's voice rumbles through the fog in my head. "She needs you, Tim. You can give her what she wants."

I look up, meet his gaze. His face is stone, but his eyes are on fire.

He doesn't blink. "You know what to do."

Do I?

Maybe.

My wits return to me slightly as the panic of indecision floods me. "But...why me?" I ask my alpha.

My alpha.

"She's not ready for me yet," he says. "She trusts you. You're the last person who ever made her feel truly loved during a heat."

"What? How do you know that?"

"I...I don't know. I just do."

Maybe he's delusional. Maybe he's hallucinating. Shit, I almost am, and their scents don't hit me as hard as they hit alphas and omegas.

But I look at her face, and maybe I'm delusional, too, because I know he's right. Or maybe I'm just a beta, submitting to the command of an alpha. Submitting to my primal instincts, letting my base, unevolved self do the thinking.

She's sprawled in the big chair, head thrown back, mouth open in a way I've never seen: like her whole brain just got wiped, and every new sensation is a foreign language she has to learn from scratch.

Her skirt is hitched halfway up her thighs, which are shaking so hard the muscle spasms ripple down to her knees. Bob is holding her hand, thumb caressing her wrist. Chris is kneeling in front of her, massive palms on her knees.

It's me she's looking at, though. The second her eyes meet mine, she makes this helpless, broken sound, all vowels and no filter.

Chris stands. He towers over us usually, but with us kneeling like this, I feel so small, like I'm some prey animal looking up to a massive pine tree. He rolls Evelyn's chair further away from the table and turns her to me.

I'm still unsure. It's been years since I've been with Evelyn like this. It's all I've wanted for years, too.

It feels like I'd be taking advantage of her. Like I'd be convincing myself this is what she wants, when it's really what I want.

She grips her abdomen, a deep pain ripping through her, closing her eyes. I slide in front of her, desperate to help. I put my hands on her calves. She jerks, but then her legs fall apart when she opens her eyes and sees it's me touching her.

She nearly whispers, "He's right, Tim. I do need you. I always have."

I let go of the fear and do what she needs me to.

I run my palms up the outsides of her thighs, slow and gentle. Her skin is as hot as a laptop running the software we use to build games in VR.

I've loved her for so long. My whole life really—before she was an omega, before I knew I was definitely a beta. The week I spent with her in her nest, protecting her, comforting her, fucking her, has made every other sexual experience, every other relationship I've had feel bland in comparison.

She's my omega. And I'm her beta. Always have been.

She's shaking even harder now, little tremors that get bigger as I close the gap between us. I lean in, the scent of her like gingerbread and electricity.

My heart is pounding so loud I worry it'll drown out her voice if she asks me to stop.

Bob kneels at her other side, offering her water, dabbing the sweat from her brow. Chris grips the back of her chair, purring, causing the whole thing to vibrate.

I draw up her skirt, just enough to bare her. I hook my fingers in the side of her panties, watching her face the whole time, and when she doesn't say no, I tug them down, slow, exposing the most perfect thing I've ever seen.

She's flushed, swollen, slick, dripping wet for me.

For us.

Ours. She's ours.

"Tim," she whispers. It's not a warning, it's not a request to stop, it's a plea to keep going. She grinds her hips forward, and my hands slide up her inner thighs, bracing her open.

I spread her lips gently, exposing her clit—an adorable little button, just waiting to be sucked. I lower my mouth, and still don't yet dare to touch her. I just breathe against her, taking in her sweet gingerbread scent. I blow gently, and the shaking that had trembled her thighs turns into a full-body shudder.

"Oh, Tim, yes," she moans out, and the last of my fears, the last of my hesitation, is gone.

When I do finally touch her, I use just the tip of my tongue, tracing the shape of her. I relish the texture, the taste of her, the way she goes taut and soft and taut again with every flick. She's so wet—dripping, just for me. She tastes like gingerbread, and I'm a man with a sweet tooth.

Bob makes a noise above me, a choked little gasp, but I don't look up. She bucks hard, almost knocking me back, but I hold her steady and suck, gentle but insistent, never losing contact. She's crying now, the sound so raw it makes my own eyes sting.

"Good girl," Chris says, and the words send another wave through her.

I push a finger inside her, slow, tilting and curling it up. Then I push some more, recalling how she likes it. I've got to go further than I think should be possible, push just hard enough that I think it might hurt, but it doesn't. It's how she wants it. I remember. How could I forget?

She clenches around me, hard, and the next sound she makes is a scream. But it's not pain, it's pure pleasure. "I remember, Evie. You like it right there, don't you?"

"Yeeesssss," she whimpers.

She comes apart, hips jerking, thighs clamping my head in place.

I keep going, not letting up until I feel her orgasm pulsing through her and hear her scream out my name again. When her body goes boneless, and quiet, I finally pull back, wipe my mouth, and look up.

She's crying, tears rolling down her face, mascara coming with it just slightly. But she looks more like she's just seen heaven than hell.

Bob is still holding her hand. His own eyes are glassy, lips parted. Chris is looking at me like I just passed a test I didn't know I was taking.

"Good boy," Chris says, and this time, the praise is directed at me.

My alpha.

I'm crying now, too. The tears come hot and stupid, but I don't care. This is all I've ever wanted: *Evelyn. A pack.* Literally every other dream I've had has just been a stopgap, a distraction. Something I had to appease the part of myself that never thought this was even possible.

Evelyn lifts her head, blinking through the haze. She reaches down and runs her fingers through my hair, slow and gentle. "More, Tim. I need more of you."

CHAPTER 19
Bob

Tim's mouth is still pressed against Evelyn's thigh when the cramps hit her again, leaving her whimpering in a chair that's now soaked through with sweat, saliva, and slick. For a moment, I think I see it: the haze of our combined scent. But it's gone almost instantly.

I make a mental note to bring the fans in here, shut the door tight, and let the filters on the fans and HVAC do their best. If the scent hasn't left the room by the time everyone returns from the holidays, there's a heat and rut cleaning service I can contact.

Maybe I'll bring this chair home, though.

"More, Tim, please," she pleads, clawing at Tim's back, trying to pull him from the floor to lie atop her. His face is still covered in her slick as he looks at her with that panic that always crosses his face right before he decides to do something. But, he lets her pull him up into a kiss that's so deep I can feel their moans rumbling through the chair where I have my hand braced.

My cock is painfully hard—like it has been all day. A condition I suppose I should get used to if I'm going to be part of this pack.

Evelyn is crying, clawing, trying to rip Tim's clothes off him, unable to get them off him fast enough. She's panicked, frantic, and impatient. A guy like Tim, one who has to deliberate as he runs through all worst-case scenarios before doing anything, moves too slowly to handle her desires. It's only a second of hesitation, but it's a second she doesn't have.

"You know what to do," Chris says. He's staring at me.

"Who? Me?" I want to ask, but I don't need to; he just nods.

I kneel beside Evelyn and speak in that tone that always reaches her, even on her worst days. "Don't worry, boss, you'll get more. You want Tim's cock, don't you?"

She bites her lip, nods, and pulls at his zipper, trying to shove him into her, but too addled to have the dexterity required.

"Shhh, it's okay. Relax," I coo into her ear and pet her cheek. "Look at you, so precious, so pretty." She nuzzles into my hand. "Don't worry, boss, this is a task you can delegate to us. We got this."

She gasps for air, the pain fully taking over her brain, and lets out a frustrated wail.

I press one hand into her upper abdomen and another into her lower back. "Breath for me, boss. You can do it."

Her pupils go into focus, and she sees me, the delirium brought on by the searing pain leaving her enough to allow her to think again. Her breath begins to return to normal, and her hands grip the chair.

Chris nearly barks at Tim, who's now standing, fumbling with his clothes, his anxiety making him less coordinated than usual. "Slow down. Breath. Just pull your pants down." Tim composes himself and does as he's told.

When Tim finally releases his dick and reveals its full length, I understand how he was able to satiate her for her first heat.

He really does have the body of an alpha.

I look at him and wonder if he is perhaps a late bloomer with his knot still buried in his gut, not having dropped yet.

I feel...so small in this moment. So...unnecessary.

What does she need me for?

Alphas aren't known for their empathy. But Chris can read me somehow, even without a bond link connecting us. He places his hand on my shoulder. "When you feel inferior, remember who just calmed her. She needs you. She needs us all."

My eyes water.

She needs me?

"You're going to help him prep her for me. Enter her with him. Make room for me." He doesn't bark. He doesn't need to. I've never wanted to do anything more in my life.

I look at his pants, his erection is flaring, and I understand why he needs us to prep her. She may be built for this, but...his dick is just as massive as the rest of him.

Chris strokes Evelyn's arms—gentle, soothing. The purr in his chest is so low I can feel it in the floor. He asks her, "You'd like that, wouldn't you, sweetheart?"

She wiggles, rubbing herself against the chair, and moans, "Yes."

Tim stands in front of her, grinning like a maniac, and for once, the worry lines are gone from his forehead. He lifts her, hugging her tight to his chest and kissing her neck, her shoulders, her mouth. He's lifted her as if she weighs nothing, and I'm jealous again. I could never lift her like that. But I try not to dwell on it.

Chris holds the chair steady, so it doesn't spin or roll away. Tim hefts Evelyn by her ass and turns to plop into the chair with her atop his lap. When Tim sits, he brings her down on his dick so easily, like it's nothing, like the two were built to fit together. She screams, relief filling her as he fills her with his cock.

Evelyn doesn't hesitate. She rolls her hips, riding out her pleasure on Tim. He leans his head back on the chair, eyes rolling into the back of his head. "Holy fuck, Evie, you feel so good," he says. Chris strokes Tim's chin, then leans down and kisses him, their tongues intertwining.

Evelyn's hair is sticky with sweat and falling in clumps around her face. I reach to push the clump out of her eye for her. Her hand finds my shoulder, clutching at the fabric of my shirt. She pulls me to her mouth, thrusting her tongue past my lips. She's frantically rolling on Tim's cock, desperate for her orgasm, and whimpers into my mouth. She pulls back from our kiss and bucks harder.

Tim breaks away from his kiss with Chris to kiss Evelyn and pinches her nipples.

"Yes, just like that," she says.

But it's not enough. She needs more. She's getting more desperate for the climax that won't peak.

I circle behind Evelyn and lean in close. I bring my mouth to her ear and inhale the sweet gingerbread before I say, "I'm going to take care of you, Evelyn."

I know what she needs.

I always do.

I was made to take care of her, and now I finally can.

I pull my dick out and hold it in my hand. It's heavy, hard, and leaking for her.

Just for her. It was made for her.

I decide to be bold and ask her, "Do you want my cock, boss?"

Tim's breath is hitching. I'm not sure how much longer he can last, but he needs to do it. He can't go limp on us now.

She turns her face to mine, eyelids heavy, lashes long and dark against her cheeks. Her lips are parted, and there's a shine to them I want to taste, but I don't rush it. "Yes, Bobby. Please help me."

The explicit request for help nearly undoes me. I love it when she asks me to help her.

I kneel up, pressing my chest to her back and wrapping both arms around her. I lean her forward, onto Tim's chest, and he shifts downward so her ass hangs off the chair at the right angle for me. "Relax, boss," I say, gently pushing her head to Tim's chest.

"Be a good girl and let him enter you, sweetheart," Chris purrs. "You'll feel better in just a second, okay?"

Chris and Tim pet her head, soothing her. She relaxes, comforted by their touch, and stops thrashing. She lies there, body trembling as tiny tremors shiver through her body.

My hands drift up, fingertips tracing lazy spirals around her nipples, and her shivers subside. "I've got you," I say, and she sighs, melting further into Tim, the tension finally leaving her body.

It takes me a moment to get to the right position, but once I do, I slide in, so effortlessly, so easily, her pussy fits to mine and Tim's like our cocks were made by pouring flesh into the mold of her. The sound she releases is so overwhelmingly erotic, I nearly lose myself.

Tim's cock twitches against mine inside her. His pulse jumps against my hands, wedged between them. "You set the pace, Bob," Tim says, leaning his head back and closing his eyes.

So I do. At first, I just hold her, swaying her a little, feeling the walls of her, and feeling the crest of Tim's cock as I thrust toward it.

I rock against her, the slick heat wrapping itself so thoroughly around my dick I can't help but rock harder. With each thrust, I can tell I'm pushing Tim deeper into her, knocking some spot she's desperate for him to reach.

I try to stay calm. I try to focus on her pleasure, but I lose myself to the sensation. Moving in and out, the sound, the scent, it's all too much. I pump harder into her, and she screams louder. "Yes, Bobby, fuck me," she wails. So I do as I'm told.

I always do as I'm told.

I'm grunting and pumping, snorting, unable to control myself any longer. I'm reduced to my primal self.

She cries out, as her orgasm clamps her pussy around my and Tim's cocks, squeezing them so impossibly tight. "Yes, Evie, that's it," Tim says. And I feel a hot gush surround my dick as Tim comes. That's all I can take.

I release into her, nuzzling into her neck, licking the gingerbread from her scent glands. It's the most amazing release, more perfect than I could have dreamed. When I come down, I collapse onto her, breathing heavy, satiated, contented, and oh so fucking in love.

Evelyn shifts and winds her arms around my neck. "Thank you, Bobby," she whispers and kisses me. When she turns to kiss Tim, I press my face into her hair, breathing her in, and it's gingerbread and clean sweat and hope.

I close my eyes, enjoying the feel of my head resting on her back, when Chris's big hand strokes my head. His purr gets louder, and he's grinning, and I know that I've done my job.

CHAPTER 20

I wait and watch. I won't take her unless she truly needs me.

I've heard enough horror stories of alphas who found their scent-matched omega during a heat, felt the sweet bliss of connection, felt the bond link forming before they even bit down on a neck, and then got kicked out of the nest the moment their body temperatures returned to normal. Those alphas walk around husks of themselves, severed from their fated mates, never able to truly form a pack again.

I shake my head, trying to remove the sorrow the thought of these three rejecting me brings.

That probably won't happen.

That kind of rejection usually only happens when an alpha forces themselves upon an omega—ruts into them without consent. But, there's a reason a contract signed by an omega while in heat is voidable: consent in that state gets...dubious.

She knows Bob and Tim. She already trusts them. They already have a bond. I can physically see it swirling around them as their scents dance together. And betas don't have the same sway over omegas that alphas do. If I wanted to, I could convince all three of them to do nearly anything. All I'd have to do is bark. My suppressant patch probably protects Tim and Bob from it, and it would protect Evelyn most of the time, but not when she's in heat.

So, I need to stay in control.

I will not lose control.

I will not lose her again.

I will not lose them.

I will be strong for them because they deserve it. They deserve my respect and restraint.

So, I wait. I watch. I wait to see if their help was sufficient to ease her pain.

If that's the case, I'll leave. I'll go to the nearest hotel with a rut restraint room and wait out the storm chained to a wall. Then, when the coast is clear, I'll come back, sign whatever deal Tim asks of me, and court the three of them properly—like a gentleman.

I don't know which scenario scares me more: the one where she needs me or the one where she doesn't.

The three of them are so beautiful, tangled together and spilling out of the chair. Tim's eyes are slightly red-rimmed from tears of joy. He wears his heart on his sleeve. I like that about him. It's cute. It also makes him an ideal packmate—no guessing what he's feeling, it's right there, all over his face, in the tension of his shoulders, the twitch of his fingers.

Bob is stroking Evelyn like she's something sacred, sitting cross-legged on the floor, his head on Tim's knee. It looks uncomfortable, but he's so blissed out he doesn't seem to feel it. He's the kind of guy who will lose sight of himself for someone he loves. I'll have to watch out for that. Make sure he takes care of himself, as well. Make sure none of us inadvertently takes advantage of him.

That's my job as the alpha: to protect them all. And protection in this day and age isn't just about keeping predators out of the nest. It's about ensuring they are protected physically, mentally, financially, emotionally. There's so much damage this world can inflict on such fragile, precious things like them that has nothing to do with physical pain.

Evelyn is limp, splayed across Tim's lap, blouse spread open, skirt pulled back down to her knees. Evelyn will need my protection, too, but I suspect she'll need protection from herself more than any outside force.

Her breath hiccups in her chest, and she looks like she may be satiated. She said she was in pre-heat, so their efforts may have been sufficient to get her through the rest of the day.

I want to ask her what her plan is. I want to know how she plans on riding out this heat. She obviously doesn't have a pack. I don't smell even the faintest trace of another alpha on her.

So, who's going to take care of her? I desperately want it to be me.

"Chris," she says, closing her eyes.

"Yes, Evelyn," I say, swallowing hard. Not daring to say anything further, afraid I'll inadvertently sway her.

She bats her eyes at me and says with a voice so sultry I feel it rumble in my balls, "Are you going to fuck me or not?"

The thing about self-control: it's a finite resource.

I kneel at her feet, next to Bob, and slide my hand up the line of her jaw. She leans into my palm, the trust in her face so total it almost undoes me. Her scent explodes out of her, swirling around my hand, and running down my arm until it kisses my neck then spreads through the room.

"Do you want me to fuck you?" I ask. My voice is gone, replaced with a low, shredded thing I barely recognize. "Are you ready for me, sweetheart?"

She nods. "Please," she says, and now I'm the one who isn't in his right mind. Because, while an alpha can bark, commanding omegas and betas to do most anything, omegas don't have to command alphas. All they have to do is ask.

I lift her from Tim's lap and sit her on the table.

She's so small. Fragile. Perfect.

She waits, patient, crossing her legs and checking her nails. The delirium that had overtaken her seems to have subsided, revealing the cool, calm, collected Evelyn who takes what she wants because she can, not because she has to. And right now, I'm what she wants. And I will give her anything she wants.

I undo my belt as Tim and Bob sit beside her on the table, awaiting her next request.

I'm not the one in control anymore. She is.

They follow her. Not me.

I follow her.

It's all for you, my sweet.

I shove my slacks and boxers down, ignoring the part of my brain that catalogs every possible disaster. My cock is already leaking, already aching, but I keep myself from rutting out—barely. The urge to claim, to mark, is so strong my molars hurt.

Bob shifts, pulling away just enough to give me room. Tim watches, rapt, his own want written all over his face. I settle between Evelyn's thighs and cup her hips in my hands.

She puts her hand on my chest, then whispers into my ear, "Just sex. Don't even think about claiming me."

"Whatever you want, my love," I say, and I mean it.

She grins, a confident, devious smile that says she knows she owns me thoroughly. "Bobby. Tim. You can rest now. Thank you." They nod and sit in chairs on opposite sides of the table. They look like they're in a meeting and she's giving a presentation on how to get fucked by a seven-foot alpha.

I line up, push in slowly, savoring the stretch, the heat, the impossible tightness of her, the way she arches her breasts forward and moans. She's so slick, and I slide in easier than I expect. The feeling is so good I nearly come. My vision goes black when I sink all the way to my knot, and her lips push against it.

I've never been with an omega before.

This is...otherworldly.

This is what all the fuss has been about.

She wraps her arms around me, pulling me impossibly close.

I force myself to hold back, to keep my rhythm gentle.

Every muscle in my body wants to go harder, faster, more.

"God, Chris," she gasps, and the sound goes right to the center of me.

I move, rocking her back, using my size to control the pace.

She meets every thrust, greedy, desperate for more. Her hands are everywhere: clutching my arms, my back, my ass. I let her take, let her have whatever she needs, because this is what I was made for.

I was made to fuck this woman.

Bob and Tim are watching—open, unashamed. Bob has his hands steepled on the table, resting his chin on them. Tim is leaning back leisurely, elbow comfortably on the armrest. There's no jealousy, no awkwardness. We're a team, working towards the same goal. And that goal is whatever Evelyn tells us it is.

I've never considered myself a submissive man. I'm an alpha. It doesn't usually come with the territory. But for this woman, I will bend the knee. I will ask how high when she tells me to jump.

Evelyn comes again, sudden and wild, and the song she sings with her moans of pleasure is the most beautiful melody—you'd think an angel was in the room with us.

She claws at my shoulder, softly bites my bicep, and then goes boneless, the tremors lasting forever.

I'm close, so close, but I don't knot her. She told me not to claim her, and if I knotted her, I don't think I'd be able to stop myself from sinking my teeth right into her neck.

She lies back fully on the table and lets me pump into her, outstretching her arms above her head. "Fuck me, alpha."

Her wish is my command. I cannot deny her anything.

I thrust into her; the sound of my dick spearing into her slick, combined with the pheromones swirling around us, is dizzying. I feel like I'm dreaming. With one hand gripping her waist, my other reaches down to thumb her clit. And just as I'm about to release into her, she comes again. Her sopping wet pussy squeezes around my shaft so hard it takes every ounce of strength in my body to pull out from her and fight the urge to knot her, locking us in place.

My seed and her slick spill out of her onto the conference table, right at the spot where I had previously sat. She sprawls backward, dozing, then curls into a fetal position.

She looks so lonely there on the table. "We should cuddle with her. Omegas need cuddles after," I say, reciting what I heard in every alpha training course I've been legally required to take since my knot dropped.

There's no room on the table for me, though.

"We should get her to her nest," Bob says.

That's a good instinct. We need to take her home. I like Bob. He knows how to take care of an omega. I ask, "Where does she live? I came here by ride share. Do either of you have a car?"

Tim says, "There's a nest in her office."

I look at him, incredulous. "She has a nest here?"

He simply nods.

I look between them and ask, "She knew she was going into heat!?"

Bob shrugs. "She's been insisting it won't happen until the New Year. I made the nest as a precaution."

Evelyn is starting to shiver; she needs a nest and warm bodies. I don't have time to express my concerns at the moment. I lean forward and pet her beautiful head. "Evelyn, may I carry you to your nest?"

She nods, but she's drifting. I can feel her going, the edges of her awareness softening.

It's all right. I've got her. We've all got her.

I lift her like she weighs nothing and hug her to my chest.

Tim straightens his clothes and walks out of the conference room. "It's this way. Follow me."

I follow him, pulling her tighter and taking the opportunity to nuzzle her neck unabashedly as I walk.

Bob gathers a few things, then shuts the door behind him, locking it with a key he has on a retractable cord at his waist.

I suppose we made a bit of a mess in there.

Her office is just down the hall, and the door is unlocked. The space smells like her. *Like home.* It's all glass and hard edges except for a couch overrun with pillows and blankets: *her nest.*

Tim and Bob pull back the layers of weighted blankets and memory foam, making a hollow in the middle. I lay her down, careful as if handling glass. She doesn't stir, just burrows deeper into the softness.

We all look at her for just a moment, then prepare to join her in the nest. Bob moves first, crawling to her side and saying, "Her next meeting is at 2 pm. We need to make sure she eats, hydrates, and has time to clean up before then. I'm setting an alarm."

Tim nods and curls up next to her.

I'm confused. I can't have heard him right. "Wait. What? She is in no state to be meeting with anyone."

They both smirk at me. "Tell that to her," Tim laughs.

I nod. "I will as soon as she wakes up. I will tell her she can't meet with anyone."

Bob winces. "Yeah, that's not going to go well for you. Lie down. Let me teach you about working with Evelyn."

CHAPTER 21
Evelyn

I must have dozed off, because a deep, sharp pain stabs me in my abdomen, and I find myself in my nest, surrounded by dudes.

I jolt upward, and I glance at my watch.

Gah. I don't have time for cuddles.

I try to stand, looking for something. I'm not sure what. Probably my phone.

"Evelyn," Bobby says, voice careful and precise. "Do you want to lie down?" He reaches for me, beckoning me back to the cuddle pile.

I shake my head, no energy for words, but lie back down, crawl deep into the nest anyway. I bury myself in the first weighted blanket I see, letting the heavy, soft cotton ground me.

I can't believe I just fucked two of my employees and a client during a pitch meeting.

But, fuck...I want more.

I can feel the heat coming off me in waves.

I whimper as my body starts to tremble.

This is so fucking humiliating.

I just got double dicked and then filled by an alpha. Why am I still so needy?

Probably because the asshole didn't do his one fucking job and knot me. I want to hire him just so I can fire him.

What the fuck was that about?

What!? I'm not worth the effort!? Not worth the time!? Too fucking good for me with your fucking perfect body and perfect smile and perfect knot?

I whimper again, this time not from pain, but from the rumination of self-doubt.

Will I ever find an alpha that won't reject me?

No. Fuck that. I don't need a fucking alpha.

I try to bury myself deeper in the nest. I want to hide. I want to die in this pile of fluff and never come out. Replace my gingerbread scent with that of a rotting corpse.

Here lies Evelyn Charles. She made a lot of money, but no one loved her.

Chris lifts his head and shifts closer to me. He's close enough to touch but doesn't—not yet. Instead, he just holds himself there, arm braced against a pillow, face intent on mine. "Do you need more, sweetheart?" he asks, voice so low and gentle.

Yes! Why didn't you knot me, you big, mean dummy?

I nod, just once, afraid that if I speak, I'll burst into tears. Or maybe flames, I'm so fucking hot and mad...and sad.

Bob and Tim move out of the way so that Chris can settle next to me. They're all moving slowly enough for me to see every micro-adjustment of their posture—no sudden moves, nothing that would spook the animal side of my brain. Chris's weight sinks into the nest, causing the cushions to tilt, rolling me into his massive, safe, warm chest.

I nuzzle my face between his pecs, and his hand hovers over my shoulder. He asks, "Can I touch you?"

It's so careful, so not-alpha, that it breaks something in me. I reach up and grab his wrist, pulling his hand to my face. His palm is rough and dry. I press it to my cheek and inhale, sucking the pine scent deep into my lungs. The effect is instant: my whole body goes loose, the muscles in my legs unclench. His fingers are callused from a life of never letting himself rest. I grip his thumb and realize he got these calluses looking for me—attending tournaments I would never show up to. I kiss his thumb, and a small tear builds in my eye.

He exhales, shaky, then runs his thumb from my lips along my jaw. The touch is feather-light, but my skin lights up.

I need him now.

I grab his other hand and pull it to my inner thigh.

I am so, so wet. It's literally dripping down my leg. My body is in open revolt against every scrap of professional dignity I ever tried to cultivate. I twist, rolling my hips toward him, desperate for friction.

He takes the hint. He shifts his weight and slides his hand up my skirt, letting his fingers tease at my entrance. He's so gentle it's almost infuriating—like he thinks he'll break me.

I want him to break me. I want him to ruin me so completely that I never have to think again.

I buck against his hand, and he finally gets it. *The big, sweet dummy.* He grins, a crooked, hungry thing, and finally sinks his fingers into me. His hands are so big, I can't tell if he's put two fingers in me or just one. I moan. The sound is high and thin and desperate. He traces up, slicking his hand, then presses his palm flat to my vulva, covering me, grounding me.

The noise I make is embarrassing, a full-throated whimper that makes Bobby and Tim shift and whimper themselves.

I grab the collar of Chris's shirt, yanking him down so our foreheads press together.

"You smell so good," I gasp.

He laughs, quietly. "So do you."

He pushes another finger inside, slow, testing, then another. Then another. And another. My pussy is so tight around his fingers, so hungry, and the stretch almost hurts, but it's the hurt that makes it so delicious.

He fucks me with his hand, gentle at first, but gradually picking up the rhythm, never losing eye contact.

"If you can take my whole hand, you can take my knot, sweetheart," he whispers.

It's so fucking filthy, so fucking hot, I shatter almost immediately. My hips convulse, thighs locking around his wrist, and I come with a violence that shocks even me. The aftershocks leave me boneless, sprawled in the nest, gasping for air.

He doesn't stop—just slows, lets me ride it out, then withdraws, licking his fingers clean. "You taste so fucking good, love." It should be disgusting, but the sight makes my cunt clench all over again.

He leans back, giving me space, but I don't want space. I reach for him, tugging at his shirt. "More," I beg, not caring how I sound.

He unzips his pants, pushing them down just enough to free himself. His cock is already hard, already leaking. I want to taste it, but the need in me is too strong—I want him inside, I want to be full, I want the knot.

He kneels between my legs, hands bracketing my hips, and pauses, waiting for permission. I pull him down, my arms locked around his neck.

He needs to stop waiting.

"Please," I whisper. "I need your knot."

He lines up and pushes in, the head of his cock forcing me open, then slides all the way in with a slow, relentless pressure. The sensation is so overwhelming I can barely breathe.

He moves, rocking his hips, and I meet him, thrust for thrust, grinding up to take him deeper.

I realize that Tim is still here. He's kneeling at the edge of the nest, hand clenched so tight I wouldn't be surprised if his nails are sinking into his skin.

I want him in this. I want all of them. I don't know if I say his name or just think it, but Tim looks up, eyes glassy.

I reach for him. He hesitates, then crawls closer, never breaking my gaze. He waits at arm's length, scanning my face for some sign.

I tilt my head back and part my lips in silent invitation. He moves, tentative but determined, and settles beside me in the nest, one hand light on the side of my head. He strokes my hair back, smoothing the sticky damp from my forehead.

I need him. I want him.

I need them all. I want them all.

Chris's thrusts get more aggressive, and the need to suck is overwhelming. I guide Tim's fingers to my mouth, sucking the tip in and biting. He bends in and kisses my temple, then the corner of my jaw, then my lips, each contact a little longer and a little less careful.

"Your cock. Now," I say, because I know Tim and know he needs to be told what to do.

The look in his eyes goes wild and grateful and so, so desperate. He shifts and frees his cock from his slacks. It springs out, hitting my lips, and I do not hesitate. I take it into my mouth and suck, relishing the taste of spiced cranberry. It's so fucking delicious, it just needs some cinnamon.

I bob and suck on Tim's cock, and my eyes search for Bobby.

Where is he?

And because Bobby always knows exactly what I want when I want it, he materializes at my side, petting my face, wiping the tears from my eyes, and praising me. "You're so beautiful, Evelyn." *At least one of them doesn't need to be told, doesn't hesitate.*

Bobby kisses my neck and tells me all the wonderful things I need to hear. His sweet cinnamon fills my nose, opening my throat further for Tim.

Chris is getting more desperate with his thrusts. The knot is there, knocking at my entrance, asking for permission to enter me. I spread my legs wider, inviting it in. Then I feel it, the base of his cock swelling, stretching me wider with every stroke. The pain is exquisite—a pressure so intense it blots out everything else. I dig my nails into his ass, urging him to keep going.

Bobby's hand has migrated to my pelvis, and he's pressing his fingers to my clit, rubbing in a circular motion, with his whole hand. *Bobby, sweet, perfect, Bobby.* I look at him as best I can from this angle, and he kisses the tear from my eye, then kisses the corner of my mouth, not caring that Tim's cock is thrusting into it.

I come again, wailing around Tim's cock and reaching up to run my fingers through Bobby's soft hair. This sends Tim, "Evie, yes!" he says, and shoots warm spiced cranberries down my throat. I grip his balls as I lick his tip clean, then lick my lips.

So, yummy.

Bobby wipes the corner of my mouth with his thumb and kisses my temple, "Good job, boss."

Tim now lies at my side, opposite Bobby and joins him in comforting me and praising me. His hand cups my breasts, squeezing my nipple in a way he learned long ago. *I remember.* I turn my head to meet his and kiss him, long, hard, thanking him for always taking care of me. Then I kiss Bobby, thanking him, too.

"God, Evelyn," Chris growls, and the sound is so raw, so animal, that I come again, clenching around him as Bobby rubs harder at my clit and Tim pinches my nipple.

Chris finally locks in, buried to the hilt, and shudders, coming in hot pulses, filling me up to the point that it wants to leak out around the edges, but it can't.

I scream. The pressure of Chris's knot is so much, so good, that I think I might actually pass out. The gentle rhythm of his huge cock and knot throbbing his hot seed into me sends me into an orgasm that lasts so long, I think my body will be stuck in this state forever.

Bobby leans in, pressing his face to the side of mine, and whispers, "You're doing so well, boss. You take him so well. You're so pretty. We're going to take care of you." But the words don't matter—it's the tone, the gentle, endless cadence, the cinnamon warmth of his breath on my cheek.

Chris lifts me, holding me, chest pressed to mine, arms cradling my head, and just rocks, gently, riding out the aftershocks until I go limp in his arms. Bobby and Tim rise, too, wrapping their arms around us and joining our embrace.

We stay like that, tangled together, joined by a knot, embracing arms, and lips on flesh. I can feel every twitch, every pulse, every heartbeat. I am utterly, perfectly safe. I hear the world as if from underwater—heartbeats, breaths, rustling of blankets.

I close my eyes. Satisfied.

CHAPTER 22
Evelyn

A deep voice pulls me from dreams of decorating a Christmas tree. "So beautiful."

It takes a moment for the world to download. First, the smells: cinnamon, pine, spiced cranberries, and...candy cane? Then, the sense of weight—three distinct varieties of it, pressing in from all sides.

I open my eyes and find Chris's arm cinched across my torso, mouth hanging open as he snores slightly. Tim is curled against the small of my back, one leg thrown over mine. Bobby is above me, cradling my head to his gut. An alarm goes off, and they each stir awake.

There's a moment of silence as everyone tries to remember who they are and how they ended up in a nest built out of my office couch and floor. There's a split second where I think: This is it. This is the rest of my life. I can lie here with them forever.

Then I remember where I am, who I am, and what is important to me.

I look at my watch.

I have meetings!

Where is my phone?

I shift, push Chris's arm off, which requires actual leverage, and sit up. I shove more limbs off of me as I attempt to button my blouse. I'm not sure why I bother; this thing needs to be incinerated. Even the best cleaners in town won't be able to get the fluids that have soaked through this silk out.

The nest is a wreck. It's sticky with sweat, slick, and semen. My phone is MIA.

I hoist myself up and stumble to my closet. I almost don't dare look at myself in the mirror.

Holy fuck, I look like I just got...well, fucked. A lot.

And well and truly good, I might add.

A smile quirks at my lip, but I don't dwell on it. Instead, I brush my hair quickly, looking around for my cellphone.

Bobby, still drowsy, joins me at the closet and assists with selecting my replacement clothing. He places my phone on the small table within it. I smile at him and he returns the smile, before pulling a jacket out of the closet and laying it flat on my desk.

Tim and Chris are still in the nest, as sleep inertia continues to affect them. Chris asks, "What are you doing?"

I reply, annoyed, "What does it look like I'm doing? I'm getting dressed."

Tim hoists himself from the nest and says, "I'll order lunch." Then he asks Bobby and me, "Your usuals?"

Bobby and I are still scurrying to get my clothes picked out and my hair in order, but we reply in unison, "Yes, thanks."

Then Tim asks Chris, "How do you like your salad?"

Chris sits up, and the nest audibly protests against his weight. He blinks at Tim, confusion marring his supposedly intelligent face. "Salad? That's not enough food for a heat."

I turn to him and snap. "I am not in heat. It is pre-heat."

Tim and Bobby smirk, and I cut them a glance that says, "shut the fuck up or you're fired."

"Evelyn, you can't be serious," Chris pleads, and I almost feel bad for him. *Almost.*

"I am serious. This is a very important day for us. The knotting you gave me should satiate me for the rest of the day. Thanks, by the way. I apologize that we weren't able to complete our pitch, but we will have to resume our discussions at a later date. Bobby, can you schedule a follow-up with Chris?"

I turn to Tim and Bobby, prepared to hand out further orders, and realize they look even worse than I do. Tim's still in his button-down, though it's lost about half its buttons and all of its dignity. He has a slick coating on the whole front of his trousers and the bottom of his shirt. Bobby's hair is sticking up in an absolutely adorable way.

I say, "Bobby, order a change of clothes for you and Tim. Charge it on your corporate card. When you fill out the expense report, please don't fucking mention anything about your clothes being ruined by slick."

Bobby just laughs at me. "Of course, boss."

I snort, and it's a relief to hear my own laugh after the day I've had.

I strip my clothes off, not worried about these men seeing me naked any longer, and shove them into the scent-masking laundry bags.

Whatever, might as well try to get them cleaned.

I watch Chris out of the corner of my eye as I dress and fix my makeup.

Here it comes. He's where he tries to tell me because he stuck his knot in me, he gets to tell me what to do.

Chris's jaw works like he's fighting to stay silent, but he just considers me and watches the three of us. There's a new steadiness to him—an anchoring weight that I can feel even with my back to him. It annoys me.

Bobby gets water from my hidden fridge. He deposits them in my and Tim's hands, then Chris's. Chris takes the water, opens it, then drinks slowly, steadily, silently, infuriatingly.

Chris stands and, without asking, gathers the scattered pillows and arranges them back in the nest. When he finds my childhood scarf, the one with foxes on it under a pillow, his scent spikes: fresh, alert, the chemical signature of "alpha is taking charge, whether you like it or not." He strokes it silently for just a moment before tucking it into the annoyingly correct place. *Who does he think he is, cleaning up my nest? My beta?*

I know what he's doing. He's trying to get me back in the nest.

Well, he can go fuck himself.

I want to punch Chris in the throat for being so predictably alpha, but I don't have the energy. Instead, I make my way to the desk and try to log in to my computer with hands that still tremble a little.

I ignore Chris and open my calendar just to ensure that neither Preston nor Finn has canceled their meetings. They haven't. Bobby, Tim, and I have less than an hour to clean ourselves up, eat, hydrate, and prep for this meeting with Preston.

Chris studies the nest, then turns and strolls toward me. He doesn't even bother buttoning his trousers, and his shirt is unbuttoned in a few locations. There's slick and semen all over him, which I pretend to ignore.

He hovers above me, standing in front of my desk, as I click away at my mouse, not actually doing anything but pretending to because I don't want to look at him. "May I help you, Chris?" I ask as cool as I can muster.

"You have more meetings today?"

"Two. One at two and one at four," I say. Now I'm typing a nonsensical note to myself, trying to look as fucking busy as possible.

Maybe I'll DM Styles. Tell her what happened.

Chris plants his hands on the desk and leans over until his face is level with mine. "And these meetings are with?"

"Clients." *Duh.*

"Beta clients?"

I do my best not to cower or smirk or sneer. I need to maintain professionalism since Chris is still a potential client. "Alphas, actually."

Chris leans back and growls, running his hand through his hair.

Bobby and Tim have been at the door, tapping away at their phone and tablet, pretending to order lunch and clothing, but obviously watching.

Chris turns to them and asks, "Bob, do you think the place you're ordering clothes from will have my size?"

Bobby stutters. "Um, yeah...probably."

"I'll give you my card. Can you get me a suit?"

Bobby nods. "Sure. No problem."

Then he asks Tim, "Does this salad place have sandwiches?"

Tim just shakes his head.

Chris sighs. "Fine, I'll take a chicken Caesar. Do they have that?"

Tim just nods.

"Great." Chris reconsiders for a moment, then says to a dumbfounded Tim, "Actually, I'll take three."

Chris returns his attention to me. I just stare at him, stunned, my mouth agape, my fingers finally stopping their fake message. He grins and says, "Well, if you insist on meeting with them, you'll need an alpha around for security. Just in case."

My words stumble, as I sputter, "But, you..."

He comes to my side of the desk and kneels in front of me. "Evelyn, you do what you gotta do. But what I gotta do is protect my pack. Will you let me do that, please?"

What the actual fuck is happening right now? That nice guy with a knot thing wasn't an act just to get his dick wet?

I look to Bobby and Tim, almost hoping they will tell me I'm on some surprise hidden camera show in which employees fuck their boss and then trick them with some weird, non-alpha-y, alpha who's fucking perfect and smells like a Christmas tree and makes you wanna cry whenever you look into his big, dumb, smart, beautiful, annoyingly sweet eyes.

I swallow and nod.

He reaches up and runs that callused thumb over my cheek, his other hand lightly gripping my thigh, and says, "That's my good girl."

My brain melts, but I resent it. So I sneer at him. Then I kiss him.

Want to know what happens when Preston Geist and Finn Future finally make it to the office? Read *Knot of Christmas Present* and *Knot of Christmas Yet to Come.*

A Note From the Author

Hello, readers! Thank you so much for taking the time to read *Knot of Christmas Past.*

While writing *Knot of Christmas Past*, my life was thrown into disarray by "an inconvenient hormone flux" (aka perimenopause). The parallels between what Evelyn and I were going through felt weirdly similar. I, unfortunately, wasn't lucky enough to have three dudes doting over me. I did, however, have a singular husband and a fresh ADHD prescription to get me through it. This book is the result of that journey.

Please leave a review of *Knot of Christmas Past* on Amazon and Goodreads.

If you'd like to keep up with my work, follow me on social media and subscribe to my newsletter:

https://www.instagram.com/imogenknowed

https://www.imogenknowed.com/newsletter

Special Thanks

I want to thank my husband for his unwavering support while I wrote this book. Without his support, I could not have hyper-focused on it, writing literally every moment of the day that I wasn't working or sleeping.

To my husband:

Thank you for enthusiastically discussing characters and plot with me. Thank you for being okay with the fact that my mind was lost to another world for a while. Thank you for always putting food in front of me when I get so lost in something and forget my own body has needs. Thank you for always being there to help me recover whenever my mind and body explode from the world being too loud, too distracting, and too scratchy. I love you.

About the Author

Imogen Knowed is a queer, AuDHD girly who hyperfocuses on creating fake people in her head. Instead of letting them stay in there, she writes them down for others to meet. She spends her days programming video games and her nights reading and writing smut. When she's not writing smut or making video games, she's hanging out with her family and pets (aka her "pack").

You can follow her on social media:

https://www.instagram.com/imogenknowed
https://www.threads.com/@imogenknowed

www.ingramcontent.com/pod-product-compliance
Lightning Source LLC
LaVergne TN
LVHW010624100826
845148LV00014B/3094